More by the author:

Lowlands
In the Empire of Dreams

The
Forest
Perilous

Book Two of the Lowlands Saga

Terence Gallagher

Livingston Press
The University of West Alabama

ISBN 13: trade paper 978-1-60489-275-8
ISBN 13: hardcover 978-1-60489-276-5
ISBN 13: e-book 978-1-60489-277-2

Library of Congress Control Number 2021930438
Printed on acid-free paper
Printed in the United States of America by
Publishers Graphics

Hardcover binding by: HF Group
Typesetting and page layout: Joe Taylor
Proofreading: Joe Taylor, Summer Earle

Cover Design: Joe Taylor
Cover photo: a-ma-seul-desire, tapesty courtesy
Musée National de Moyen Âge (formerly Musée de Cluny)

This is a work of fiction. Any resemblance
to persons living or dead is coincidental.
Livingston Press is part of The University of West Alabama,
and thereby has non-profit status.
Donations are tax-deductible.

6 5 4 3 2 1

The Forest Perilous

Book Two of the Lowlands Saga

Preface

The Forest Perilous continues the story begun in *Lowlands.*

Lowlands tells the tale of James Ward, a high school fresh-man living in Queens. On his way home from school one day, James makes the acquaintance of Cornelia Parsons, a girl a little younger than himself, and finds an entry to a strange new world.

James learns that Cornelia and her guardian, Vivien Wid-dershins, are members of a loose confederation of travelers, wandering "tribes" with roots in Ireland and Britain, who live according to their own law and without much regard for any other. They are remnants of the Jacobite exiles who left for life and service on the continent centuries ago. A few of these disappointed exiles chose not to assimilate, but instead turned to a gypsy lifestyle. Miss Widdershins, as queen of the Dragons, the oldest tribe, is the preeminent authority among them. As young James is drawn into the life and troubles of the tribes he discovers an unexpected family connection to the Dragons through his deceased grandmother.

In the end, the Dragons disappear as suddenly as they arrived. James is left alone; he dreams of the day when he will be reunited with Cornelia and resume his life with the Dragons.

The Forest Perilous begins seven years later ...

1.   *Departures*

1.

We begin again in the month of May, following my graduation from college. May, when as the book of the Knight Prisoner sayeth, "Every harte florysshyth and burgenyth and lovers callyth to their mynde old jantylnes and old servyse." For the first time in sixteen years the summer opened up without the inevitable and dreaded finale of school doors closing behind me again in the fall. For the first time in that long, long while, I didn't know where I'd be at the end of the summer.

If I were wiser in the ways of the world, I might have been more worried than elated. I had not put myself in a strong position leaving college, as one of only two majors produced by the venerable Classics department of a "Little Ivy" college tucked snug among the hills of Massachusetts. Most of my classmates had jobs lined up and careers plotted out. Not me. A century before, my degree might have suited me for all kinds of occupations, from a man of letters to a foreign officer to an ad man, or at least not disqualified me out of hand. As things stand now, it was hard to see what the world would allow me to do, other than teach the useless subject I'd learned, and that would mean years more schooling.

Well, I'd done it to myself and there was no one else to blame. I wasn't worried; not about that. I had other things on my mind, other hopes to sustain me and other problems to solve. Though I had not heard a word or a hint from them since the day they left half a gold ring in my mailbox, it was my full determination and purpose to find Cornelia and the Dragons. I knew where I was going, though I didn't know how to get there.

It was seven years since I had seen Cornelia. She might have changed a great deal. I didn't think I had changed at all. I was the same child I'd always been. Everything I had done over the last seven years, every path followed and decision made, had been done shadowed by the knowledge that as soon as I was able I would take to the road and find the Dragons again. I had no reason to be certain that this was even possible, but I couldn't imagine what else I could do with myself. It was time to seek a roving life, along with the raggle-taggle gypsies.

It wouldn't be easy. My mother was so glad to have me back after four years at college, I knew she would be upset when I left home again so soon. They made it awfully pleasant for me that summer, nice easy days with ice cream and gin and tonics on the porch and reading in the yard. They put no pressure on me to run out and get a job immediately. I guess they figured it would take me a while to 'find my way.'

My father made a few of his typical 'suggestions,' which start out as suggestions and end up as warnings: "You might consider coming into publishing if you don't mind starting out with peanuts. And ending up with peanuts. I could talk to some of the people at my outfit to see if they have any openings or internships. I don't know. The business is changing fast. It's all technical now. They've farmed out the manuscript reading and editing to agents. See how long that lasts. Well, people are becoming less literate, aren't they? Ever heard of SEO, search engine optimization? When people write, they select words purely with the intention of attracting search engines. They're already using it for advertising and marketing. Soon they'll be using it for the books themselves, for fiction. Soon books will be written by computer programs. You think I'm kidding?"

All of which was entertaining, but not likely to spur me to action.

My lassitude scandalized my more hard-charging relatives when they came over to celebrate my graduation. Here I was, given the opportunity to attend this famous old New England school, and I seemed ready to fritter it all away. I suspect that secretly they resented what they believed to be my undeserved luck — I'd won another scholarship — in contrast to how hard their own kids had to work. I played up my lack of ambition and disaffection for my own amusement.

"You've got to seize the day," said my cousin Cheryl. "This is the time for you to spread your wings. This time of your life will never come again. What do you *want* to do? Do you want to teach?"

"Only with a gun to my head."

"Teach in Colombia," said my passing father.

"Why do you say that?" asked cousin Cheryl, still addressing me. "Your sister teaches. Doesn't she like it?"

"Not from what I've heard."

My sister was inside the house and couldn't be reached for comment.

"You're only young once, and believe me it passes fast. This is the time you should be on fire, you should want to go out there and change the world."

She turned to my grandfather, who was seated beside us on a lawn chair, passing in and out of awareness as he sat. I recognized a kindness, my cousin trying to include Grandpa in the conversation.

"Uncle Raymond, don't you think young people should want to save the world?"

It was an ill-chosen conversational gambit, coming as it did from a world of ideas that was totally closed to my grandfather.

"Eh? Save the world? Who?"

"Young people. The young. Didn't you want to save the world when you were young?

"Me? No." My grandfather laughed gently. "No."

Her daughter chimed in, fresh off a miniseries about World War II and the Greatest Generation, I'd guess.

"But Uncle Raymond when you went off to fight the Nazis, didn't you want to save the world?"

My grandfather laughed again, amazed.

"No. Save the world? No. I just wanted to go home in one piece."

Later, and for a long time, he kept returning to this and shaking his head.

"What was that? Change the world? Save the world?"

"A little of this, a little of that."

"Who wants to save the world? These people I see, in the

street and on television, do they think they're going to save the world? Why? How?"

At this stage of life, he had taken to repeating himself. I could only keep telling him I didn't know.

2.

I was very lucky in that I had no student debt. My scholarship took care of most of my expenses, and my parents' generosity, supplemented by my job washing dishes in the cafeteria, took care of the rest. Also, aside from books, I had almost no expenses at college. I wore clothes until they wore out. When I wanted entertainment I went for a walk in the hills. I had no car, so I made no trips and bought no gas. Practically speaking, I graduated at square one, with no debts but with a degree that would earn me no money. But four years older. A perfect James Ward performance, one might say.

Now that I was free to pursue my quest, the lack of an automobile was going to pose a problem. As a matter of fact, I did have a car promised to me whenever I was ready, Troll's old Mustang, but I didn't have a license. I hadn't learned to drive. Not really surprising, considering I spent the bulk of every year up at school. I figured that even if I managed to get my license over the summer, I'd forget how to drive over the other three seasons.

Troll's Mustang. He never did get to drive it much. He'd come home and drive it between deployments. He used to drive over to my house sometimes and we'd play ping pong again. He seemed more or less the same, only maybe a little preoccupied. I never asked him about overseas and he never told me much. Why would he? What would I understand? Our life had always been a matter of vacations and visits, slow-maturing jokes as we lay on the cool lakeside grass and listened to the evening crickets. There was too wide a gap to bridge between that old easy life and the hard rock and hot sands of his new calling. He'd just tell the occasional funny story, mostly about basic training — an inexhaustible source — and about life with his buddies back on the base.

Now that I think about it, however hopeful its beginning, May ended on a sour note that year. Aunt Joanna had asked us to accompany her to a Memorial Weekend ceremony out on the Island. I had been to such ceremonies before and I did not like them. Bereaved family members, usually a mother and sister or a wife and daughter, stood at the podium reading out the names of the slain. So Aunt Joanna and Uncle Joe were going to stand there and say "Eugene Mazza" and somehow that was supposed to make everything better. And all the while there were the guys on motorcycles with beards and bellies and many little medals, veterans I can only say *swaggering* around because they had made it and Troll hadn't. It was an irrational perception on my part, I suppose; almost everyone there had lost someone. But it was the way I felt. And when I say felt, I mean really felt, in my gut, like a twisting invasive fist in my stomach.

But as my mother said, "It helps your Aunt Joanne," and that was enough.

When the day came, it was as I had feared. The reading of the names, the only feeble ceremony our society seems able to agree on, sounding querulous, like a series of complaints. Then the speeches, how they had died defending our freedoms. Troll had been killed on his third deployment, while on patrol in a town he had also patrolled on his first deployment. I don't know what he was defending at that point, but I'm sure he did it well. Then came the defiant ones, who stood at the podium and addressed the terrorists, how our resolve would not be broken, how we would hunt them down, how they didn't understand this country, how we would never surrender. Safe in the cocoon of a Long Island town on a sleepy long weekend and not a terrorist within six thousand miles, to the sound of applause and whooping. It embarrassed me. It bothered me too because it seemed to validate Troll's death, to declare it necessary and good, and I didn't think it was either. My being there implied that I was one of them, that I thought as they did.

My mother was right, though. Our presence did help my Aunt Joanne, and my Uncle Joe too. Even more they were helped not so much by the ceremonies, but by standing together with the other bereaved, talking or not talking. Troll was their only child and they had long lives of grief stretching before them. They needed this, and my reservations were a small thing in comparison.

As it turned out, my attendance at the ceremony even helped me, as I saw one thing there, wholly unexpected, that I wouldn't have missed for the world. A *Waffenghoul* t-shirt, one of the last of its kind. *Waffenghoul* was Troll's band, a crazy affair he'd started even before he entered the Marine Corps, that existed on and off on three continents, through peace and war. The kind of music they played depended to a great extent on what instruments they happened to have with them. When pressed, Troll described it as "death folk." They played everything from German folk songs to a heavy metal version of the Baywatch theme. As a matter of fact, the back of the *Waffenghoul* t-shirt proclaimed "The legendary Edge of Surrender tour" with a list of nondescript venues which included at least one café that had been blown apart a few years back and still lacked a roof.

The band and that t-shirt in particular caused Troll a lot of trouble. The band's logo was printed in exaggerated heavy black *fraktur* script across a red background and the jagged ff of the *Waffen*, with the light cross bars of the f, looked uncomfortably like the SS logo from the bad old days. The American armed forces frown on any display of the paraphernalia of Nazism and Troll was called on the carpet and asked about it more than once. The thing is, he couldn't explain the name without violating the band's sacred code. His protestations of innocence fell on skeptical ears.

He wouldn't even tell me what *Waffenghoul* meant, just gave me a couple of hints.

"You took German in school, right?"

"Right."

"The W is pronounced in the German way, like a V."

"OK."

"You know I'm half Italian, right?"

"Yes."

"That's all the hints I'm going to give you. Know or not know. It's up to you."

Eventually I figured it out.

The t-shirt may even have had a hand in his death. Troll believed that his smart-assery had retarded his progress in the Corps and held him back at least one grade. If he had been promoted as he otherwise deserved, maybe he would not have been performing that particular duty on that particular patrol. Death was all over the place over there, though. Maybe they would have found some other way to kill him.

Regardless, I was happy to see the old logo, and walked up behind the wearer.

"*Waffenghoul!*" I said.

He turned, surprised.

We shook hands.

"Were you in the band?" I asked.

"I played guitar and 'auxiliary instruments.'" He cocked his head. "I don't remember..."

"I'm Troll's cousin."

"Oh, right, you must be Ward."

We talked easily. I could imagine him as one of Troll's buddies. I sensed in him some of the same skepticism that I felt about the memorial ceremony, overlaid with other emotions that I couldn't experience.

After a while, he said, "Are Troll's parents here?"

"They're right over there. I'll introduce you."

Their meeting was a small joy to help heal a great sorrow. They all knew what to say, unrehearsed and genuine, but with a certain strange elegance. It was knowledge gained at great cost.

That's how May ended for me. I was reminded once more of the affair a couple of weeks later when Aunt Joanne mailed us a story from the local paper, a story that featured a photo of a Korean War veteran, some guy who hadn't been killed, with that faraway look in his eyes that they always wear for the camera, in an old uniform with many medals on his chest. That annoyed me all over again, but only for a little while.

3.

Then June came and with it the first letter, and my adventures began in earnest.

I had stopped by the Big House already, once or twice. It looked like it was going through one of its fallow periods. No answer when I knocked, and the lawn cut by an unseen hand once a month. I tried some desultory research on the Internet, but I couldn't think of what to search on. The killing in the field had never been solved. I searched on Travelers (and Travellers), Tinkers, and Gypsies, killings with swords, manuscript discoveries. I searched on names. Nothing.

I was just beginning to research property deeds in New York — maybe I could get a line on the householder — when the Dragons, again, anticipated me.

It was a Saturday morning and I was puttering about in my bare feet with a big mug of coffee in my hand. A shadow passed across the windows on either side of the door. Something bigger than a squirrel was on our front stoop.

I pushed out onto the landing and heard small shoes slapping against tar. When I walked down the stairs I saw a little girl with long wavy hair running away down the driveway toward a waiting car. She looked fearfully over her shoulder; she was obviously performing a spy operation. She saw she had been caught and dove into the back seat.

I raised my coffee cup to her. Spy or not, she was a little girl. She waved back and smiled. The car drove away.

I walked up the stairs and reached into our brass mailbox. There was a letter waiting for me, just as I suspected and dearly hoped. To my surprise, it was not from Cornelia but from Miss Widdershins.

Four before Kalends of June
Dear James:

They tell me you have graduated from university. Congratulations.

As you know we left you very abruptly and without a proper farewell. That has weighed on me. We would like to offer you our hospitality now. We are in our Northeast Summer quarters and will be for the remainder of the summer and probably until winter falls. They are in Pennsylvania, not so very far away from you. Let me know if you would be interested in a visit, short or long as you please, at a time of your choosing. We can map you a route or arrange transport.

Cornelia and some Cats are encamped nearby, so it would be a happy reunion.

We can communicate in the usual way.

Tell me, how is your grandfather? A fine old gentleman.
Vivien Widdershins

I drafted three responses, each shorter than the last. I wound up writing a short note to the effect that I would be happy to come out and visit the Dragons and Cornelia, that I supposed it would probably be in July or August, but that, alas, I did not drive. I folded the note into an envelope addressed to Miss Widdershins and popped it into the box. Now the focus shifted to dealing with my parents.

I knew they would be disappointed that I wanted to take off almost as soon as I got home, especially my mother, and I knew that they did not trust the Dragons, especially my mother. She never forgave them for moving away without warning, although she gave Cornelia a pass, figuring that, as a child, she had to go where she was taken. Legally I was old enough to go where I wanted, of course, if I could find the money, but none of us subscribed to the theory that adult children are free to act with no regard for the feelings or wishes of their parents. Ours was not a legal or financial relationship; love and respect must have their due and the affair must be managed according to their dictates.

I had already told my family about the tribes and the Dragons, after a fashion. I did not mention the defection of Con Gone-Away, or the battle for the painting, or the fight in the park, but I told as much as I could. I framed them as Travellers, a familiar enough concept, who perhaps tread a path closer than most to the margin of illegality and sometimes step over it. I told them of the tribes' descent from the Wild Geese, a point strongly in their favor. I did not go deeply into the differences between the tribes or into the Dragons' claim of an earlier origin and a descent from a more ancient king. It was hard enough for them to believe what I chose to tell them. I think it would have been impossible if they had not themselves met Cornelia and seen the others.

The clincher came when I revealed our family connection to the tribes through my deceased grandmother, a Dragon born and bred. They pressed my grandfather for confirmation. He did his best. He did well. He wandered over the same ground many times, supplying new details now and again, answering my father's questions about long gone relatives.

My sister pored through fifty-year-old photographs: "Him, is he one of them?" She struck pay dirt with a little square black and white picture of my grandparents sitting at their old kitchen table (which we still had out in the garage, pushed against the wall with the unscrewed legs taped to the bottom). Along with them sat two spare bold-eyed men in dark jackets and narrow ties, wearing hats indoors. One of them held my shaky toddler father up as he stood in his white baby shoes on the table.

"Those two?"

"Yes. They were your grandmother's cousins."

My father chimed in. "These two I remember. They used to visit us quite a lot when I was little. Then they stopped; I think they moved away. They only came once in a while after that. The last time I saw them they brought me my violin."

So I had already done a good deal of the spade work. But how could I reintroduce the tribes into our lives? I decided to build on our recent correspondence. It had been a sore spot with my mother that neither Cornelia nor any of the others had written to me. I would alter that perception.

"I've heard from the Dragons," I said. "We've written some letters back and forth."

"How long has this been going on?" asked my mother.

"Just this year."

"They waited long enough. Did Cornelia write?"

"No. Just Miss Widdershins."

"Mmmm."

"Where are they?" asked my father.

"In Pennsylvania somewhere."

"Where in Pennsylvania?"

"I'm not sure."

My sister asked, "How do you write to them, if you don't know where they are?"

"They move around a lot. I don't know exactly where they are at this moment."

"Uh huh."

"That doesn't seem very fair," said my mother.

"Are they planning to move back to NY?" asked my father.

"No, I don't think so."

"Mmmm." My mother was not impressed.

I left it at that. Baby steps.

It was ten days before I got Miss Widdershins' next letter.

June, three before the Ides

Dear James:

So glad you would like to visit us. Now we must find a way for you to get here.

We are tucked away not far from the Pfalzheim area. I am not familiar with rail or bus transport; it may be onerous finding a route. It may be more advisable for you to wait until we can find someone from New York to give you a ride.

There is another possibility. A couple of our people are doing the festival circuit on the east coast. They are finishing up at a Renaissance Festival of some description in Ulster County. After they are finished, one or both of them will be driving straight back here. Perhaps you will be able to ride with them. Does that sound feasible?

Vivien Widdershins

The date was a puzzler. Roman reckoning. It seemed like a pointless affectation.

Much later Cornelia asked me, "When you get letters from Aunt Vivien, does she do that thing with the dates? The ides and calends and all that stuff?"

"Yes."

"They've been doing that since forever. A royal prerogative, I think. No one knows what they're talking about. It's pretty annoying."

I had a copy of *Kennedy's Latin Primer* so I could figure it out. The date was June 11. I got the letter on the 15th. I had put my own letter in the box late on June 6th. That worked out to be a four-day turnaround allowing one day for writing.

I had initially thought the letters were passed from door to door by hand, but that did not appear to be the case. There must have been no regular traffic between New York and Pennsylvania; otherwise when it came time to visit, I could have hitched a ride along with the mail without bothering about the Renaissance festival. As near as I could figure it, they must mail the sealed letter to someone living in the vicinity who then carried it over to our box. I'm not sure why they didn't just mail it to us directly. Maybe they wanted to keep my family out of the loop. Or, more likely, maybe she sent over a lot of correspondence in one package, and this was only one piece among many. She did, after all, have a kingdom to govern.

I worked on my reply again. I'd prefer a car ride to public transport, if possible. I could get up to Ulster County by bus. Was the Renaissance Fair the one being held at the end of July?

When I went out next morning to put the letter in the post, I found the little longhaired girl already on the porch, standing on our cement planter, getting ready to go fishing in the box. I handed the envelope directly to her. She smiled at me, took the letter without a word and jumped down the steps, then stomped off down the driveway.

Miss Widdershins kept to the 4-1-4 timing. I found the next letter on June 25th.

11 before July Kalends

Dear James:

Colin will be at the Renaissance Festival. I have told him to look for you. The festival lasts three days, from Friday July the 16th to Sunday the 18th. I would suggest you arrive on Saturday, so as to be sure not to miss him. He will be manning a blue booth and selling handmade jewelry. You will recognize one another. You can travel to Pennsylvania with him immediately after the conclusion of the festival.

We will be very glad to see you again. We will be staying in the Northeast Summer quarters until the cold weather comes. Cornelia, too. You can stay with us, here or elsewhere, as long as you like.

Vivien Widdershins

That much was settled. On the home front, however, things were not yet well. My mother did not take the news lightly.

"Who is this Colin person? Do you even know where you're going?"

She paused, then ran over my stammering reply.

"These people have been operating for six years without any trace of them. Not a trace. Don't tell me you didn't try to find them. You haven't heard a peep out of them for six years, and now they show up with no phone number, no address, not even the name of a town where they might be living. Just an 'area.' And you're supposed to go off with this unknown booth person, God knows where."

"No," raising a hand to forestall my father. "How do I know that I won't see you for seven years if you run off with these gypsies?"

I didn't have much of an answer, only to assure her that it was a short visit, while she laughed in angry skepticism.

I didn't like leaving my mother in such a state. I swallowed my pride and sent another letter to Miss Widdershins outlining my mother's objections. She came from a hierarchical, family-based society, I reasoned — she'd respect the need to reassure my mother.

In response I got an honest-to-goodness letter from Cornelia, complete with stamp and return address listing town and PO box. It arrived fast, just before the July 4th holiday.

June 30 Roman Martyrs

Dear James:

I'm so glad you're coming to visit us! You'll get to meet my mother too. We're just up the road from Aunt Vivien. You'll love the Dragons' Sun House in the woods. They've been using it for two hundred years. We're just in trailers, up the road, as I said, but we use it all the time. I have a summer job at a stable taking care of the horses and taking people on rides in the woods. It's called Woodland Rambles Horse Farm.

I hope all your family is well. Please greet them all for me. I would love to see them again, when I next come out to New York.

Cornelia

4.

$\mathcal{T}his$ last letter helped a great deal. I gave it to my mother. She
kept it for a while, holding the envelope in her hands and running
her thumb over the edge. It allayed her panic. She was reconciled
to my going now, but she still asked her same questions.

"How long are you planning to stay?"

"I don't know. It's just a visit."

"Where will you be staying? Do they have a room for you?"

"I don't know. I'm bringing a sleeping bag just in case."

"How are you getting back?"

"I don't know. I can probably get a ride from someone passing
through New York. Worst comes to worst I can take a train from
Philadelphia. I'd better bring some money."

She even took unaccustomed refuge in practicalities.

"Have you given any thought to looking for a job? Did Dad
suggest anything?"

"I'll start looking when I get back. There's no sense before
that."

Packing for the trip was difficult. I decided to bring only my
big frame backpack. It lay on my floor for a long time as I shuffled essentials into it, then reshuffled them among the clever little
pockets and nettings and tie-ons. It wasn't designed to serve as a
suitcase, but I knew it would be my most flexible and easily portable option. I tried to keep the weight down. I wasn't much of a
camper but I had at least learned enough to be realistic about my
capacity as a beast of burden.

As the day approached I started feeling uncertainty about the terms and the purpose of my visit. Maybe my mother had sowed doubt. I'd been dreaming of reconnecting with the Dragons for years now, but now that it was about to become a reality, I found myself confused. What did I expect to happen? What did they expect? There was nothing to do but let it play out.

Once, through a closed door, I overheard my father reassuring my mother.

"Look at it this way, he's just visiting a friend he hasn't seen in a long time."

My mother was unconvinced.

"I'm sorry, I don't trust those people. I don't want him wandering all over the country with a lot of gypsies. I want him to come home. I want to see him again."

My father went on in a soothing voice, telling her not to worry, that I was "sensible," that I wouldn't do anything foolish. He was being reasonable — or pretending to be — but my mother saw deeper and clearer.

When the day came to leave, we all played it low key. I was just going off for a little visit, nothing special. My heart lightened as I walked to the train station. I have always liked going away — just the simple act of going away without any regard to what I was leaving or where I was going. I rode the train to Penn Station, then walked up to Port Authority. The big backpack was awkward in the thick New York crowds. I had to twist and sidestep and block the pack to one side or another, reaching back with my arm to do so.

Port Authority was its usual unlovely self. It had improved a great deal since the old days, so my father said, but it was still a dreary place. It was a good way to leave New York because it did not tempt me to stay. I was as much an alien here as any Dragon.

I had a long wait. I bought a newspaper, finished what little reading I could endure within fifteen minutes, and spent the rest of the time watching people. At last the bus was ready and the luggage bays were opened. After my pack was safely stowed I climbed aboard, instantly reminded by the sickly sweet unidentifiable smell how much I dislike bus travel. I leaned my head against the window and watched our slow progress out of the dark ugly station and up the spiraling escape ramp.

I was on my way.

2 Arrivals

1.

The bus dropped me off in a gravel lot in front of a roadside diner. It was a little muggy, but I was grateful for the fresh air. I hadn't yet eaten the sandwich in my pack so I went inside and bought myself a nice lunch. When I paid the check, I asked the waitress if there was a place I could call for a cab. She showed me a number pinned to the wall near the entrance. I should have asked before I ate; it was a long wait before the driver showed up.

I figured the festival was three or four miles away. I asked the driver but he had no idea there was a Renaissance Festival in town. I pulled out the brochure, printed off the internet, and he recognized the park it was being held in.

He didn't like Renaissance Festivals and told me so. I could see he was a man who had to tell you what he thought about everything. This was unnecessary, because one could guess within five minutes of meeting him what he would think about any given subject. Not a man of surprises. I supposed that he disliked festivals because they gave pleasure to parents and their children.

He dropped me off in the crowded venue parking lot. I must have been one of the few to arrive in a cab. From the lot you couldn't see any of the hoopla — it just looked like a busy day at the park. I walked up the long sloping concrete steps, and I began to hear strains of music, and the rustle and ring of many voices. In contrast to my horseless carriage driver, I loved outdoor festivals.

I emerged from the sheltering trees and stood in line at the entry booth. With my hand stamped and a festival map-and-program clutched therein, I stepped with the others onto the charmed ground. I thought I'd wander around for a while before looking up my Dragon contact. It was labeled a Renaissance Fair — Faire actually — but it was really a potpourri. Cotton candy, a petting zoo, step dancing, weaving exhibitions, flower shows, games of skill and chance. It was as if everyone who hadn't made it into one of the big festivals, the ones that advertise on television, was bundled into this one. It was perfect.

The layout was interesting. The park was obviously not designed for festivals, so you had to walk a long path from one attraction to another, even over a little bridge. It must have been tough going for the fat-bottomed and the elderly; there were a number of whirring electric minibuses to assist them. It was tough going for me with my heavy pack. I consulted my guide frequently; I didn't want to spend much time backtracking wrong turns.

I saw on the schedule that there would be a joust before the king in just fifteen minutes, followed by an exhibition of weaponry and dancing. I detected a wash of spectators flowing away to the east. I thought for a moment to join them, but when I compared the surrounding topography to the map, I saw that I was standing close by Vendor's Row. It was here that I would find Colin the Dragon, and here I should stay.

Foot traffic at Vendor's Row was light and getting lighter as the festival attendees hurried off to see the jousting. In the booths, the vendors were taking a break, stepping out of sight behind their pavilions for a little alone time, or hanging out by the posts and guy wires, talking to their neighbors. In her last letter, which I had unfortunately lost, Cornelia had said that Colin "looked like an old hippy." I saw a couple of possible hippies, but none that was a possible Dragon.

I started paying closer attention to the wares. I was on the lookout for jewelry and metalwork. Toward the end of the row, I found what I was looking for, a lot of gold and garnet and colored glass. It looked like someone had put Sutton Hoo on display. As I ran my eye over the finery I became aware of a figure in the dark recesses of the booth. It was not Colin the hippy, but a woman, a red-haired woman sitting in a tipped chair, with bare feet propped on the edge of the counter. She was taking a few puffs on a clay pipe and looking at me critically.

I stopped. We both looked. She spoke first.

"Ward?"

"Yes."

She rose and walked to me. We shook hands. She was little and tight-bodied and didn't look like she'd aged much in the seven years since I'd seen her last. She was the woman who'd fixed Cornelia's hair on St. John the Baptist's day and who rolled the ring to my grandfather's feet that day in the park.

"Come around," she said, and held the back flap of the booth open for me.

"You can drop your pack," she said when I stepped inside.

"I'm Siobhán. I remember you from New York."

"I remember."

"Interesting times. Colin's off fetching food. It's too bad you didn't get here before he left."

"I have a sandwich."

"Och, a sandwich! They have good food here. Vendors get half price. He usually buys too much. I'm sure there'll be some for you. *Feic,* here he comes."

Colin came balancing food in an open box. Cornelia's description of him was not inaccurate, but incomplete. He did indeed look a bit like an old hippy, with his long grey ponytail, wandering moustache and lean body. There was something different about him, though, something more, something I only put a name on after I got to know him better.

He stepped sideways through the gap into the booth and looked for a place to lay his box, slipping it onto an inside shelf below the display. We made introductions and shook hands. He was not a large man but had a grip on him.

There was food for me as Siobhán had surmised, a meat pie, always welcome. We sat on stools and picked through the hot steaming meat and pastry. They liked their food but didn't seem to need much of it.

As we ate I complimented their wares.

"Yeah, he does good work," Colin said. "I help him with a few of the smaller pieces."

"You *do* a few of the smaller pieces," said Siobhán.

"But the really choice stuff, the big stuff. That's top quality work, that's beyond me. It's almost too good for the circuit. We have to price it accordingly and most people, when they go to these festivals, aren't ready to spend that kind of money. Some days we make more from Siobhán's music than from the jewelry."

I looked over at Siobhán and noticed for the first time that she was wearing a period dress with a sort of grey silken sheen. She could have been wearing one of those tall conical hats with trailing veil, that medieval staple from the picture books, and it would not have gone amiss with that dress. She saw my perplexity and pointed with her pipe across the display to the left. I rose to look and saw, next to the main booth, a smaller wooden installation almost like an old fashioned ice cream cart, piled with musical instruments both wind and string, prominent among them a small harp. A stool sat by the cart and a can by the stool, and a fluffy pile of loose bills threatening to spill out of the can.

"*Ceol is seoda*," she said, "music and jewelry. The music is supposed to bring the buyers in. But most days I make more than he does."

"You attract the wrong element," said Colin. "Cheapskates."

"It was ever thus."

We ate at leisure, finishing with baked goods, two raspberry tarts split three ways. Colin insisted. Then the people started to drift back from the jousting and demonstrations, and Colin and Siobhán prepared to receive visitors.

"Late afternoon is usually slow. But that's when people make the big purchases. There's something they saw, and they thought it was too much, but they've been thinking about it all day, and they know if they don't buy it now they'll never have another chance, so they come back to our booth at the last."

I stayed with them till closing and got to hear Colin's *spiel* more than once.

"People like to feel a connection with the artist," he later explained to me. "We tell them it's a family enterprise."

"Which it is," said Siobhán.

The artist lived in the mountains of North Carolina. There was an explanatory flyer tacked to the corner of the booth, with a black-and-white Xeroxed picture of a cherubic old man in a workshop. He was too old to make the trip, Colin said. He told people that he was the artist's apprentice. He explained the process of making, old world craftsmanship, bronze, gilded silver, cloisonné, champlevé, colored glass and wire. Only a few people bought, and only the smaller pieces, but he was satisfied at the end of the day.

Siobhán cranked out the awning from her little cart, tipped her harp back and played, sitting on the stool. She played airs on a fiddle and what sounded to me like troubadour songs on a series of recorders.

Once she asked me, "Do you play anything?"

Honesty compelled me to admit that I had studied the bagpipe in college, and I was relieved that she had nothing analogous to the pipes in her bag of tricks.

After lunch wore off, she stepped into a pair of shiny grey slippers and laid out on the grass a few squares of interlocking wooden flooring with foam backing. She played some sprightly simple tunes on a tin whistle, while doing a slow jig with lots of turns. She had grey eyes, a swinging red pony tail, and a wiry graceful body and many stopped to watch and to listen. The men especially stopped to pass a few words. She did well enough too when the money was counted at the end of the day.

2.

They were the last to close up shop. As the afternoon wore into evening, and the faire-goers moved to clear out the parking lot, most of the other vendors started packing up and were already finished by the time the faire officially closed its doors at 6:30. Colin and Siobhán only started folding up their gear at that time, but they were very efficient, packing the pieces away in velvet-lined cherry-wood cases which they stacked and stored. Siobhán folded her handheld instruments up in a long thick cloth that served as a case, expertly positioning them so that none touched the others and all were swaddled safely.

Siobhán had made a last minute run to the food court an hour and a half before closing, so we managed a satisfactory feast, pulling lumps of tepid spicy stew out of Styrofoam bowls with plastic spoons. I sat with the others on a blanket spread behind the booth. I wondered if I should chip in for the food, then surmised, correctly, that I was to be treated as a guest. Colin brought out some unlabeled bottles of stout. We took a long while over our meal, reclining afterwards and looking up at the thickening cloud cover.

Siobhán had music in her blood, it seemed. More than once she started a tune, humming at first then ripening into song.

I told her, more to make conversation than anything else, "You should sing, too. At the faire, I mean."

She shook her head in a definite fashion. I understood; the

songs were for us only.

At last she rose.

"It's going to rain. We'd better sleep in the booth. I am going to wander while I have the chance."

I wasn't sure what she meant, but it appeared she meant what she said. She simply walked off into the park and disappeared into a stand of trees.

I gathered our debris and walked it over to the trash, then continued to the lakeside restrooms. Colin had told me they kept the facilities open as a courtesy to the vendors. We weren't the only ones who stayed with our wares throughout the night. On the way back I passed a few deer walking out of the woods to graze. They flapped their ears and stood at attention but did not startle. When I got back to the booth I saw that Colin had unrolled his and Siobhán's sleeping bags on the trampled grass inside the booth. I realized he intended to go to sleep and that the two of them probably had the grisly habit of rising and setting with the sun.

The dark fell fast. I unrolled my own sleeping bag and climbed inside. I couldn't imagine how I'd fall asleep; I was normally good till midnight. Siobhán slipped back in the booth and hung her grey dress against the wall. I heard the rain start slapping against the roof.

"Are we going to need the tarp?" Colin asked.

"No," said Siobhán. "We should be OK."

Soon they were breathing easy. I closed my eyes, then opened my eyes. I listened to the rain drops and tried to separate sounds and detect patterns. I ran over the history of Super Bowl matches, starting with Packers-Chiefs. I reconstructed Mets lineups from years ago. I tried to recite poetry to myself, as my grandfather did when he had trouble sleeping. Just when I thought I'd go crazy, I woke up.

I was alone in the booth. I sensed motion around me, so I popped my head up. Some of the other vendors had arrived and were beginning to set up. It was still early for me, but not for others. I scrambled off the top of my sleeping bag (it had been too warm to stay inside) and began rolling it up. As I was stowing it in my pack I saw Colin and Siobhán approaching. They looked like they had just been laughing about something.

"Thanks for watching the booth," Colin said.

"No trouble."

"Cornelia's a great sleeper, too," said Siobhán. "She's a hard one to wake."

I remembered that was true; she had slept through the assault on the Big House seven years ago. Seven years, almost to the day.

This second day dragged. So long at the faire. I couldn't really help them with anything. They told me to walk around the faire grounds and enjoy myself, but that palled after a while. It was a big park and if the weather had been nicer I might have taken a long walk, but the air was humid and thick. I waited in the long line for refreshments and brought lunch back for all of us, forgetting that as vendors they could have gotten half-price if they'd gone themselves. They did not mention this as many another would, only thanked me for the food. I was glad to do something.

I did get to see the jousting and the swordplay and the dancing, sitting on the ground and plucking grass, alone among all the families. To my relief, the last day of the faire was shorter than the others, ending at five. When I got back to the booth Colin and Siobhán were in high spirits. One of the big pieces had sold, a gilded bronze eagle inset with semiprecious stones.

"It's kind of a Saxon piece," said Siobhán. "He's doing a lot of Saxon jewelry now. The Celtic stuff has fallen a wee bit out of favor. Well, it had a good run. Most people think the Saxon stuff is Viking. That's all to the good. The Vikings seem to be very popular now."

Siobhán went off to satisfy the business end of the proceedings with a thick sheaf of receipts folded into a leather purse. Colin disappeared for a while then came back driving a pickup truck pulling a two-wheeled trailer.

I helped Colin pull the booth apart and stow it in the trailer. It fit together like a puzzle. Most of it went into the trailer, together with Siobhán's ice-cream cart, which broke down into flat planks and a folding wheel assemblage. It seemed there wasn't a cubic inch of free space in the trailer when we closed it up and locked it down. We slid a few of the longer planks and posts into the truck's flatbed. The instruments and wares also went into the pickup, not in the flatbed, but in the cabin, in the back seat.

Siobhán came back.

"Everything set?" Colin asked.

"Yep. Let me sit in the back for a bit."

We climbed in. The cab smelled of tobacco, but not unpleasantly. It took a while before we steered free of Vendor's Row.

Some of the other vendors were still loading up. On their way out, Colin and Siobhán waved at their colleagues in a friendly enough manner and received waves in return, but everyone resisted the urge to chat. Without being obviously standoffish, they had very effectively kept to themselves over the last couple of days.

It was only when we turned out of the park and onto the main road that I shook my mind free of the faire and remembered where I was. I was driving with Dragons, headed back to Miss Widdershins and the girl who'd left me behind.

3.

It was a long slow trip. One of those days when the traffic snarl-ups create ripples that spread and join others and find their way into every main artery leading into and out of the city. The first jam, three lanes squeezing into one, broke just before we reached New York. We sailed through, running on a new hope, but soon after we hit Jersey the vise closed again.

"Unbelievable."

Colin was a man of few words. He stared sadly out the window and drummed his fingers on the dashboard. He hardly needed to hold the wheel, only to tread on the gas when traffic lurched forward from time to time.

"We should be there already."

Once I heard Siobhán singing in the back seat:

Mary Pickens on a wall
Mary Pickens had a fall
Mary Pickens very tall

Mary Pickens dancing

Colin was looking in the rear view mirror with a smile on his face.

"She sings in her sleep," he explained.

I had no idea what relationship obtained between these two. Were they married, inamorata, siblings, cousins, or merely co-workers? I didn't like to ask. Maybe it was their life as outsiders that had conditioned them or just their natural courtesy, but personal questions were not part of the Dragon style.

When he'd had enough, Colin pulled off into a rest stop.

"I gotta take a break. Who knows, this might clear up by the time we get back on the road."

It was a relief to stretch our legs. It was dark and getting late, but the stop was still fairly crowded, as Colin was not the only driver who had decided to step out of the slow stream of traffic for a while. We were a motley group. We were on the High Road from Canada to the Deep South and there were drivers and tourists from all over the country and beyond. Out by the parking space, in the comparative darkness, were the dog people, letting their poor beasts run for a few blessed moments. As I approached the big main building, lit within and without brighter than day, I was reminded irresistibly of those disreputable trading posts where the heroes used to stop in the crazy post-*Road Warrior* movies of the eighties. Outside the structure there were wheeled double-decker carts and booths displaying wallets and leather goods, potted herbs and flowers, sunglasses and watches of dubious worth. Inside were eateries of all descriptions, from fast-food joints to bakeries with pretensions toward elegance. Everywhere there were people milling, vacationing families newly revived by food, groups of teenagers running up and downstairs, and a few people who looked like they might be transporting bodies in their trunks.

Siobhán and I split some sort of delicious chocolate covered crepe. Colin made do with coffee and a donut. After we had eaten and hit the crowded restrooms, we took our time getting back to the car, strolling about the grass near the parking lot and slapping bugs. When we got back on the road, it seemed to me that the traffic had thinned a little.

I zoned out for the rest of the trip. We still had some heavy traffic on heavy roads, skirting Philadelphia, then we were suddenly on smaller, darker roads walled by black trees. Colin knew where he was going. It was late when we turned off the public highway and took a path without lights or markings. Colin stopped at the foot of a house with lights along its open porch. The surrounding woods were black. The clouds hid the stars. He left the engine on and waited.

A woman came out on the porch. A big dog tried to run past her to the car but she ordered him back on the porch. He was wagging his tail and gave out with a yip or two.

"Colin, *awill tusa ann*?" she asked.

"It is."

She asked something else, and Colin answered. "He's here. The three of us."

"Rooms are ready in the bunkhouse. Do you need food?"

Colin looked around at us. The others weren't hungry, so I went along with them. I still had my sandwich if I got peckish.

"There's a fridge in the bunkhouse if you get hungry or thirsty. It's late — I'll let you sleep. Mr. Ward, we'll give you a proper welcome in the morning."

Colin waved and headed farther up the road at a slow pace. It wasn't long before we pulled up before a low building, dark except for a single light burning above the door. I carried my backpack in; the others left their belongings in the car, including the cases of jewelry. The door to the bunkhouse was not locked and we walked in without knocking.

Colin switched on a light. The bunkhouse was neat as a pin. The front door opened into a small anteroom, a sort of common room with easy chairs, a refrigerator and a sink. A narrow dark corridor led away straight toward the back. We weren't hungry, but we were all thirsty. There were glasses in a cabinet above the sink and we found a full gallon of milk in the refrigerator. Between the three of us we finished the better half of it.

"I'm turning in," said Colin. "If you need it, you'll find a bathroom at the back of house. There are three bedrooms off the hall. Sleep as long as you like. Give me a knock if you need anything. I'll take the first room."

He turned on the hall light. The whole bunkhouse looked to be constructed of smooth, close-grain wooden planks fitted seamlessly together, giving off a delightful soothing perfume of cut wood. One after the other Colin and Siobhán peeled off into their respective rooms. The low wooden ceiling of the corridor and rougher, creaking planked floor gave one the impression of being on a ship.

I stepped into my cabin and felt for the light switch. It was a perfect room, only a bed and a side table with a lamp for reading. No closet but a free-standing clothes rack with a row of empty wooden hangers. A small chest at the foot of the bed for I don't know what. Very much like a cabin.

I had done little that day but wait, yet I was quite tired. When I turned out the light and sank into the soft pillow and my eyes grew accustomed to the dim light, I saw that the room was not windowless, as I had thought, but was lightened by a small window just under the ceiling. My porthole. I could lie and watch the unfinished darkness of night shining through the glass and casting its image on the wall. At length, I closed my eyes. I don't think I've ever had a better sleep.

I never did eat that sandwich.

4.

When I awoke, I lay listening to the birds outside the window changing their voices moment by moment. There was no other sound, not a person, not a car, not a leaf blower or lawnmower. I didn't know the time. I assumed it was late.

I carried my shoes in my hand and creaked down the hall in my socks. I didn't know if Colin and Siobhán were still asleep or long gone. I pulled on my shoes in the anteroom and opened the door. I didn't pause long but it was long enough for a big furry dog to appear and face me. He looked like a big police dog, except for his color which was a dark, almost gunmetal grey. He looked very intelligent and regarded me with a concerned frown. We took stock of one another. I knew I wasn't going anywhere the dog didn't want me to go.

Maybe I had picked up the scent of the bunkhouse, maybe he was used to strangers staying there, whatever the reason he accepted me as a friend. He gave a high yip, turned, and ran off down the road.

I walked past Colin's truck and stood on the road he'd driven along last night. To the right, I knew I'd find the first house we'd passed. To the left the road narrowed to a footpath — there was a chain suspended from two posts to block any overbold cars.

I followed the path left. I was surrounded by trees, great heavy trees set far apart. Where I went to college, there were woods all around us, and I used to go walking at all seasons of the year, but they were new woods, most of them, thinner and set closer together, still in the process of reclaiming lost land. Often I would find the stone foundation of an abandoned farmhouse among the trees.

This was the deep dark forest. These trees looked like they had been here always and had never been disturbed. When my father read Grimm's fairy tales to me in my childhood, these were the woods I saw in my mind's eye. I could not imagine where we were or how we had gotten there, so close to the big city, as I thought, and so far from its power.

The path was sloping upward now. At length, looking up the trail down the long leafy tunnel, I saw brightness ahead, announcing a clearing. When I got to the end of the path, a funny little freestanding crooked wooden gate blocked my way. There was no fence attached and I could easily have stepped around it, but I carefully opened it and then shut it behind me, before I stepped out on the bright grass.

I was on the broad sunlit summit of a long low hill. There were no trees here, all was in meadow, stirred by a pleasant breeze. The grass was long on the margins but mowed neatly throughout the center. Dominating the view was an open rectangular building, founded on stone with a peaked roof supported by mighty rough-hewn wooden posts. This, I thought, must be the sun bower of which Cornelia spoke.

The wall at ground level stood solid as the wall of a castle, a rock wall constructed of very large heavy stones, mostly grey, fitted together and mortared. It only rose a few feet; above it the structure was open to the sun and wind; the green tile roof was supported only by the posts, at the corners and at key places along each of the sides. The far end of the sun bower only was enclosed, and that was by red climbing roses woven throughout a white lattice.

I climbed five steps up into the structure. There were many ways up and down, little flights of steps arranged around the three open sides. The floor was raised above the level of the grass, thick unpainted planks, very dark and old-looking. The bower was empty. Where I stood, in the center, I could smell the scent of the roses brought to me by the wind. I listened and I thought I heard something. Not voices, exactly, but a low far murmur that made me think voices might be speaking.

I walked down five steps and stepped out onto the grass on the bower's other side. Looking across the field to the far end, I saw them, a family, together in the quiet of the sunshine. There sitting on the grass was the yellow-haired queen and her dark consort and champion, and between them, not sitting but hanging on each of them, with a hand at their necks and swaying comically from side to side, was a newcomer, a little boy, the future king of the Dragons.

3. Royal Welcome

1.

His name was Arthur. He was a sturdy little fellow who very much favored his mother in coloring and build. I had little experience of small children and I could only guess at his age. I found out later he had recently celebrated his fourth birthday. He was not an especially chatty child even then, but always interested in what others had to say. He greeted my advent in silence, though he did shake my hand when prompted. The first words he spoke to me, when we all four of us passed out of the field back down the wooded lane was, "Did you come through the gate?"

Miss Widdershins looked older and stouter and even a shade darker, as if from many days spent sitting out in the meadow under the sun. She had kept her beauty and her regal bearing but, though I hesitated to express it this way even to myself, there had grown up something of the buxom barmaid about her. The merry crows' feet had spread from the corners of her eyes, the lines at the corner of her mouth had deepened, there were silver threads among the gold, and she seemed happier than I remembered, happy in a way that made itself felt physically by those around her.

He, Thomas the Rhymer, had changed less obviously. He was large and solid as ever, with a little of the grey badger now in his close-cropped hair. When he looked at me though, I no longer heard in my mind's ear the menacing drone of far-off eternal battle as I did in the old days. He seemed abstracted, like a man lost in a dream with no wish ever to leave it.

They were happy to see me. They told me Cornelia would be happy to see me. Arthur, once through the gate, ran ahead down the lane. On the way down, Miss Widdershins again took the trouble to apologize for their long absence.

"We thought it best to leave after the unpleasantness with Con Gone-Away. And then, after our split with the Geese, New York became less of a haven for us. I have not returned to the city for many years. Such foolishness. We lost a great deal from that divorce. As indeed did they. Well," she threw her hands up in a resigned gesture, "at the least we have remained friends. It will all be explained to you later."

The rest of the walk back to the houses was occupied in unexceptional visit-talk. Arthur was waiting for us back at the bunkhouse, with his two hands clutching the fur of the big grey shepherd. The dog frowned up at me with an expression I soon grew to recognize. He always looked as if he was saying to himself, "Now where do I know this fellow from?"

The distance from the bunkhouse back to the first house, which served the purpose of a sentry box, was shorter than it had seemed in the dark. As we approached, a figure rose from the porch; not the woman who had greeted us the night before but a figure well remembered from the past. It was Balin, standing guard once again, laying down his cigar on the arm of a rocker and walking to the edge of the steps. He hadn't changed at all, it seemed.

"We're going up to show James the town," Miss Widdershins said.

Balin nodded, then addressed me with a faint smile, "You again. Welcome back."

We took a perpendicular road to the right, narrow, hard-packed gravel, a little weed-grown at the edges. We walked in the shade; the tree branches almost met overhead. Only a hundred yards up this road we came to a high gate built into a red brick wall, two square pillars on either side with a little peaked roof spanning the gap. The gate itself was black wrought iron, swung back on both sides and bolted into the ground. We stepped through this onto cobblestones. The "town" proved to be all center — a town square with no town, just a thin line of houses, shacks and trailers surrounding an oval of cobblestones. Some of the houses looked old, long-settled residences with bright red flowers sprouting from window boxes. Some looked like workshops, board shacks with barn doors standing open. On the right side, farthest from the front gate were some trailers, and tied to one a pony pulling at the long grass.

I didn't have much time to evaluate any of this or to pick out details, because we walked straight through. We were going on to the castle. At the other end of the town stood another gate, an exact replica of the first. I couldn't see, but I could guess that the whole assemblage of buildings was surrounded by the brick wall through which the two gates opened. Once through, we were on another narrow path, too narrow for a car, with a stone floor and high walls on either side. The path climbed and curved to the left and when I passed this curve I saw yet a third gate waiting, and beyond it I could just peek into a sunny courtyard.

This third gate was even more impressive than the first two, taller, built of stone and with an honest-to-God portcullis pulled up on chains. I couldn't imagine what had prompted them to build such a thing, except that they could and there was no reason not to. Cornelia had written that they'd lived here for two hundred years and it was obvious that they'd taken the time to make themselves at home.

The castle was something of a mott-and-bailey arrangement. A high stone curtain wall held the world away, high but not thick since it was not needed for physical defense. Inside, to the left of the gate, a neat little house pressed up against the wall, a white cottage surrounded by lavender. This, I learned, was where the royal family actually lived when they took up their Northeast Summer quarters. Across from the gate stood the keep, a massive round building, not very tall, built thick like a keep should be. The top floor was open and flat and crenelated, for looks rather than archery. Even with the dragon banner flying from the top, it was not visible from the nearby road because there was a wooded ridge that stood as a natural barrier. I don't know if it was visible from anywhere outside the grounds, except from the air.

As we approached the castle gate, Arthur ran ahead and by the time we stepped into the courtyard he was climbing into a large faded plastic car. He was already a little big for it, and its wheels slipped rather than rolled across the cobblestones, so he moved it by standing up inside it and hauling it around. He spent a great deal of time simply sitting inside with a big smile on his face. It was sort of his own castle within the castle.

It was a cozy life within those walls. I got to know it fairly well over the weeks to follow. When the sun on the stones grew too hot, the royal family would take refuge in the central garden, a stand of gnarled fruit trees that dropped their bounty on the bench-sitters below. Along the northern wall grew carefully tended vines, from which was produced every year a very small amount of ice wine. Arthur's toys were littered throughout. Flowers and vines climbed all along the inside of the wall. Breezes and blooms, birdsongs and bumblebees — a cozy life, and unguessed by outsiders.

I had thought at first that we were far off in the woods of western Pennsylvania, isolated by distance from the hustling world outside. In fact, we were not so very far removed from the urban centers of the East. The ancient forest, which had stood without disturbance since the days before the arrival of Columbus, occupied a few hundred acres acquired by the Dragons in the long ago. Their property was their defense, and their wealth too, as I later learned. When they needed to deal with outsiders, with the county or with tradesmen, they did it through the first two houses, the guard and the guest houses. These made an acceptably normal show; they were fully wired for electricity, which the Dragons extended to the other buildings or supplemented from a generator when the need presented itself. Except on days of celebration, the Dragons rose and set closely following the sun, which minimized their need for electrical power. Their drinking water they drew from a pair of artesian wells, which had not failed in living memory. It was a hidden kingdom, at peace among a thousand enemies.

It had lasted this long but I wondered how long it could last. The nets were drawing tighter all around.

2.

Later that day, as perhaps he saw time hanging heavy on my hands, Colin asked me, "Do you want to go to town with me and pick up supplies?"

There was to be a gathering that evening, at least partly in celebration of my arrival.

"We can swing by the stables and pick up Cornelia on the way back. She's got a part-time gig there."

The trailer had been unhitched from his pickup and the covering was off the cargo bed. I climbed inside the cabin; the seat was already beginning to seem familiar. We started back down the road to town. I must have passed this way the previous night, but I didn't remember it. We hadn't gone more than a few miles when Colin slowed and turned up an even smaller side road.

"Let me show you something."

Within a few hundred feet he pulled off directly opposite a sun-dappled maple-lined lane.

"There, up there. That's where the Cats are camping."

I must have sat up very straight, because he reminded me, "Cornelia's not there. Still at the stable. We'll pick her up on the way back."

We pulled a U-turn and returned to the main road. We passed clear through the first noticeable town we came to, and just at the outskirts turned into the parking lot of a surprisingly large shopping center. It must have serviced the whole area. The bright lights, high ceilings and conditioned air, not to speak of the uniformed employees and rows of well-stocked metal shelves seemed strange after even one evening in the Dragon's kingdom. I felt as if we had entered a space center, as if we were on an expedition of some kind.

Colin knew his business and hit one store after another, rapidly filling his cart or basket as the occasion required. He paid in cash. He showed an ID at the liquor store, though he was clearly of age. I noticed he had a driver's license but I didn't see what state it was from. I noticed that he did not pass any chit chat with the cashiers and I also thought I noticed hostility in the looks of some of the shoppers and workers. I couldn't think why. There was nothing especially provoking about his appearance or conduct. Maybe they knew him and his associates? Or maybe it was just a new paranoia on my part.

We loaded his purchases, mostly food and whatever was related to its preparation, in the truck bed and secured it with netting. Then we were back on the road. I quickly lost sense of direction as the country roads bent and branched, rose, twisted and fell.

We came to earth again in a wide concrete driveway, a small parking lot really. The big wooden sign at the entrance said Woodland Rambles Horse Farm. When we parked I could see into a great big open barn with horses visible in the shadows and all around fences and fields where other horses grazed in the sun. Some parents were bringing a happy little skipping girl back to their car, parked close by Colin's truck.

Colin knew the place. He led me toward the barn. We navigated the usual hazards, attended by fearsome buzzing horseflies. When I stepped under the shadow of the barn I lost my vision for a moment and had to wait until my eyes grew accustomed to the darkness. I stood in the entrance and looked inside and saw a young woman crouched checking the right front leg of a big patient animal. Then she rose and addressed the horse.

"You're fine, you're just lazy" and kissed it fondly on its hairy cheek.

Then she saw us.

"Hey, Coll. Are you picking me up?" she said. "Is it time already?"

She saw me.

"You! Is it you? Colin, take the reins."

She held them out and let them drop, then came over to me.

"It is you. You came."

She gave me a big strong hug then held me at arms' length.

"Look at you!"

I looked at her. She was very tall, taller than I. She had the same crazy hair, grabbed back by a band the same old way, and about the same length. She was not so skinny as she had been. She looked like an athlete. With her big shoulders and long legs she looked like a 50 meter swimmer. She was dressed in jeans and boots and some kind of western-looking shirt, pulled across and secured with large buttons. She looked fine.

I said something or other. Neither one of us was really listening, only looking.

"Let me bring Berry back to her stall. I'll be a few minutes, I've gotta tell Katie I'm leaving."

She took the reins from Colin, who had picked them up of course, and began walking the complaisant horse deeper into the shadows of the barn. She was talking to Berry now, conversationally, but I couldn't hear what she was saying.

Colin and I stood aside to let others bring horses in and out. Blacks and bays, dapples and grays. Such big powerful beasts they seemed, but so patient, so generous.

When Cornelia returned and we all climbed into the pickup, she sat in the back seat and leaned forward between us.

"So what are you all doing? What brings you out here?"

"We're picking up supplies for the shindig."

"Ah, the 'shindig.' James, you'll get to meet my mother. A terrifying woman."

"We're going to stop at the market on the way back."

"There's a farmer's market just past the campground," Cornelia explained to me. "I'll go with you."

Colin navigated the roads expertly but, I noticed, at a moderate speed. He observed all traffic regulations. The Dragons did not deliberately draw attention to themselves.

"So did you call your mother and tell her you arrived safely?"

"Oh! No, I forgot."

"You thoughtless, thoughtless young man."

"I'll do it when I get back to the Dragon's."

"You can't. They have no cell phone reception. And no phones."

"I can't do it here, I don't have my cell phone with me."

"Thoughtless."

Cornelia shook her head gravely and leaned back in her seat.

The way back seemed faster than the way out. We were soon driving past the Cat's leafy lane, which Cornelia pointed out to me. A couple of more minutes up the road and we pulled into the lot of a farmers' market. Colin grabbed a couple of baskets and waded in.

Before she joined him, Cornelia extricated a cell phone from the back pocket of her jeans and handed it to me.

"They have reception here. Call your mama! Be a good son and call your mama!" And she was off into the market.

We still had the generic answering machine message, a deracinated male voice intoning, "At the tone please leave a message." I started talking, and after a few seconds my mother picked up the phone. She was indeed glad to hear from me, and encouraged by what I could tell her about where I was. I could hear my grandfather in the background. When he divined that I was at a farmer's market, he told my mother that I should see if they had strawberry rhubarb pie. By the time I hung up, I was very glad I had called.

They carried out two big baskets each, mostly produce along with jars of honey and jam. I had found Grandpa's strawberry and rhubarb pie in a white box and carried it out as my contribution to the party. We loaded the baskets in the back seat next to Cornelia, who was into the peaches by the time we reached the campground.

"Under ripe," she commented. "It's too early."

When we let her out she took off up the lane and through the speckled leaves like a child returning home from school.

Back at Dragon Town, as I thought of it, they had already set up some long tables in the square. Colin drove straight through the main gate and parked on the cobbles. Townsfolk had emerged from the houses and sheds and were busy stringing lanterns, straightening table cloths and setting up what looked like a serving station. Some I recognized from the old days, most I didn't. I saw Balin walk past on the edge of the square. He took no part in the labor. He was concerned with one thing only, and it wasn't preparing food. Cornelia had once said that his was a hereditary role. The last knights of Europe, perhaps, he and his brother.

After Colin and I unloaded the food and the other supplies from the truck, I found myself without an appointed task. I left the others at their work, work they obviously knew well, and walked back to the bunk house for a late afternoon nap.

3.

They sat me next to Cornelia in the middle of a long table, one of two, covered end to end by overlapping linen tablecloths. Siobhán had awakened me from my nap by rapping on the door with a knife handle and calling, "Come out, come out, the guests are here, the food is waiting."

I came as I was. I had no choice, really, as I had only brought the bare minimum of clothing, whatever I could fit in my pack. It was in the gloaming, already dark along the path under the trees, when I arrived at the square. The lanterns were lit alongside the tables. People were milling about, some already seated.

It was there I met the "terrifying" Mrs. Parsons, Cornelia's mother, who revealed herself to be a small, thin-featured, rather Scottish-looking woman, whose eyes narrowed to slits of amusement when she smiled, which she did frequently. She came over to greet me, with Cornelia in tow.

"Well, well, James Ward, at last, at last," and seized my hand with both of her own.

We sized each other up with ill-concealed curiosity. I don't know what she saw or concluded, but I saw a woman with few obvious similarities to Cornelia. Small, comfortably proportioned, neat, smooth-haired, rather proper in demeanor — she presented quite a contrast to Cornelia. Although I was a bit wary of her penetrating gaze, my heart warmed to her as it became obvious how proud and how fond she was of her unruly, long-limbed daughter.

Mrs. Parsons battened onto my arm and obliged me to walk her to the table when it was time to be seated. Cornelia sat on my left and Mrs. Parsons on my right. It was obvious that this, and the rest of the seating at the table, was according to design, though I was not sure how it was accomplished. There were no name plates. Maybe the others already knew their places. The other table seemed to be a bit freer in seating and manner than ours, and I thought I detected a bit of a class differential between the two. At our table sat the royal family, the guests of honor, Balin and some of the others I recognized from the old days back in Queens, the soldiery, so to speak, and their wives. At the other table sat those who cooked the food and brought it, those who strung the lanterns and cleared the board at the end of the meal. Siobhán and Colin sat among them. It might have been a case of birds of a feather rather than a function of class distinction. If it was the latter it did not seem to be an oppression. After all, everyone sat to eat and drink, and when it came to dancing at the end we all danced together.

Arthur had decided that the fun was with the servers and he insisted on staying by the serving stations and "helping." They wouldn't let him handle the hot food, but my half-filled goblet was brought out to me, with great concentration and pride, by the future king of the Dragons. What do they say, *"togha gach bia agus rogha gach di"* or vice versa, "the choice of every food and the pick of every drink"? We ate like kings all, and the food was hearty and savory, stews and chops with grilled vegetables and fried potatoes with fruit and pie to finish. I didn't taste the half of it, though I tried.

It wasn't easy for me to follow the conversation, seated as I was between the two Parsons women, talked at and across from both sides. Mrs. Parsons showed a surprising interest in my education.

"Cornelia tells me you're just after graduating from college. Tell me, what was your experience of the place? Would you say that you enjoyed it?"

I didn't enjoy anything that involved dealing with an organization of people, or having to be at a certain place at a certain time, or reading and thinking on schedule, but I recognized this as a flaw in myself not in the institution. There were things, people, events that I liked at college, so not wanting to give Mrs. Parsons an unjust impression, I said, "Yes, it was all right. It was up in the country, in New England, a very nice setting. And I did learn some things."

"Do you think it was worth the effort? The time and the money?"

"That's a tough question. I didn't spend much money; I was on scholarship."

Mrs. Parson nodded sagely.

"Scholarship. Very good. Do you think the experience was worth the time spent?"

"That's another tough one. What else would I be doing? I guess it was worth it. A college diploma is almost a necessity ... or it's treated as a necessity ... for a lot of jobs nowadays. Although I guess that doesn't really help me much; I majored in classics."

Mrs. Parsons considered my tangled and self-contradictory answer.

"Was it wrong to major in classics?"

"Well, it's not very practical. It doesn't have any obvious application to a job. And frankly I think it angers a lot of people when they hear about it."

"How odd."

"The reason my mother is asking these questions," Cornelia leaned in on the other side, "is that there has been some talk of me going to college, or at least a two-year community college to start."

"Really?" I was surprised. More, I was dismayed. Even shocked.

Mrs. Parsons explained.

"We wonder if it would help Cornelia more easily make her way in life if she had a college diploma of some kind. Although none of us ever needed such a thing in the past. Still, it might keep some doors open to her." Then, as her mind wandered down a parallel road, "Do you know she had to fill out paperwork to get her position with the stables? Pages of it. It almost prevented her employment."

"And I but a humble stable girl. See, we're developing a plan. If I go to a 2-year school first, and do OK, I can switch to a 4-year later. And you know how we're planning on paying for it?"

I shook my head.

"Volleyball! You can actually get scholarships for playing volleyball!"

"Do you play volleyball?"

"I went to a couple of camps. They take it so seriously! You wouldn't believe it. The coaches yelling and everyone clapping hands and hugging. Anyway, I'm sure I could make a team." She continued, "You know, I don't understand it. People, that is Belly-men, strangers even, are always telling me about how important it is to go to college, like it's something magical, like it will expand my mind — 'spread your wings,' that's what they say — and it turns out I can get in because I'm tall and can bop a ball over a net. Isn't that odd? I think it's odd."

"Sports are big at some places. Not at the college I went to. Although, come to think of it, I think they may have had squash scholarships." I squinted, trying to remember. "Is that possible?"

"Too bad they don't have professional volleyball," said Cornelia.

"Well, there's beach volleyball."

"Eh, what's that?" Mrs. Parsons was startled back into the conversation. "They play on beaches? Is that out west in California?"

My head was pingponging between the two of them. When I looked back at Cornelia she was staring at me with urgent eyes and shaking her head subtly but rapidly. She explained later, "If mama ever saw the costumes they wear in beach volleyball she'd bust a gasket."

I eased out of the volleyball talk, and we rowed merrily along until dinner gave way to dessert. At this stage of the meal, empty seats began appearing around our table, as people got up to stretch their legs or to visit friends. The seats opposite myself and the two Parsons stood empty as often as not, and guests started coming over to introduce themselves to me and pass conversation with us, Cats as well as Dragons. I noticed a certain quality in their looks and their smiles, a sort of shy inquisitiveness, an archness in some of the women, and it began to dawn on me that Cornelia and I were being treated as an item. I was Cornelia's young man come a-courting. Even at that early stage, I dimly guessed that this new status carried some social constraints along with it. There was to be no more wandering free at our own whim for Cornelia and me, as we did in the old days. Our courtship, if such there was, would be carried on under the watchful eyes of both clans. It reminded me of the Sicilian sequence in *The Godfather,* with Michael and

Apollonia trailed by the whole village. It was a bit of a nuisance. A charming nuisance, but a nuisance nevertheless.

We were all sated and drowsy. Arthur slept soundly at the head of the table, no longer helping as the last of the plates was whisked away. Dolores was at his side, the old nursemaid with a new generation to care for. I was alone at the table, Cornelia and her mother having gone roving for the moment, and I sipped my after-dinner port and looked at the stars. The scrape of a fiddle drew my attention earthward again. I saw that the Dragons were in the last stages of piecing together an interlocking wooden floor, like Siobhán's festival stage writ large, over a broad expanse of cobblestones between the tables and the second gate. It was for dancing. I did not want to dance. I never danced at college and I had no idea what the steps here would be. I would be content to sit and watch.

Siobhán tapped me on the shoulder.

"Come on," she said, "Let's go."

"Sorry, I'm not really a dancer. I don't dance."

"Can you walk?"

So food-addled was I that I took this to be a genuine inquiry about my health.

"Oh, yeah, sure, I'm fine."

"Then you can dance."

"But I don't know any of the steps."

"It's easy to follow, especially the first dance. I'll show you. Look, you are not going to sit here on your duff while Cornelia is up there dancing. Let's go."

I had to laugh. She led me to my place. The whole village was there. We stood in a wide circle, men and women alternating. Any more of us and we would have circumscribed the wooden floor — as it was, when we broke into lines the dancers at the ends found themselves on the cobbles. The fiddle scraped and the tune began. It fascinated me, that instrument; bigger than a violin, its tones carried over the whole company. Soon it was supported by a plucked instrument and what looked like a hurdy-gurdy.

The tune was not what I expected; slow, stately, it sounded neither Irish nor Scottish, but like a troubadour's Spring song.

"Just follow me," said Siobhán.

I learned a lesson there about dancing, that if everyone else knows what they're doing it's really not that hard for a newcomer to slot in. We started to turn, the whole ring and each dancer turning in place, then back again. A woman standing by the dancers began to sing. I could not guess the language. It sounded like Latin half-way along its journey into a Romance language. It was beautiful. I heard Siobhán at my side singing along. I saw Cornelia across the circle, head inclining this way and that with each step.

We broke into lines, danced across and back, then the leaders of each line passed in weaving motion down to the other end. I took Cornelia briefly by the hand, smiled into her flushed and shining face, then traveled past. Still the music and the song went on, and we stepped it out slowly and courtly. It could have gone on forever as far as I was concerned.

There were other dances that night, to other tunes and other

4. Matters of Law

1.

A few days, it may have been a week, after the big welcome party, I was summoned to the castle by Miss Widdershins. Dragon Town had been quiet in the interim; I was beginning to get a feel for the routine of the place. It made me realize how noisy it was back at home in Queens, between the cars rushing by too fast on the street in front of my house, the lawnmowers and leaf blowers working the neighboring properties during the day, audible for blocks, and the airplanes crossing the sky overhead day and night, audible for miles. To say nothing of our own contribution to the noise, the TV and radio, the window air conditioners and dehumidifier in the basement, the dishwasher in the kitchen. Even the refrigerator made a grinding noise from time to time, letting us know that its labors were getting to be too much for it. At Dragon Town there were no such distractions; life carried on very much as it had for centuries, with the only sound and music produced by direct human or animal agency, or at the pleasure of the wind and the rain. There were exceptions, of course; sometimes an unusually fast or loud car made itself heard from the far off unseen road, sometimes a prop plane buzzed overhead. These occurred rarely enough that they provided a welcome, brief diversion.

What excitement there was during the week was provided by the departures and arrivals of the townsfolk, which usually took place in the very early morning or late evening respectively. Despite their long-established brick walls and stone paths, the Dragons still lived a roving life, and the population of the town changed from week to week. The first thing new arrivals wanted to know was which of their friends and relatives were there before them.

In fact, my summons to the castle was delivered by Colin on his way out of town. I'd seen him loading up the truck the previous night. He brought me to my door just after dawn with a sharp insistent knock. I was getting better, but I hadn't yet adjusted to the early hours that the others kept. When I finally opened the door, I saw he was packed and dressed for travel.

"I'm for the road," he said. "I wanted to say goodbye before I left."

He stuck out his hand. "Do you think you'll still be here when I get back?"

"When will you be back?"

"Four weeks. Maybe five. We're swinging by North Carolina then up through the mid-West."

"I don't know. I don't really know how long I'm staying."

"Maybe you'll find out something today. The Lady asked me to tell you to stop by the Castle this morning. She wants to talk to you."

"What time?"

"I don't know. She didn't say. Shoot for noon. Well ... hope to see you again. *Slán is ádh*. Health and luck!"

"*Slán*."

I walked to the front door to see him drive off. He left with

Siobhán in the passenger seat and a man I didn't recognize seated in the back, wearing a black wide-brimmed hat with a high crown. I had learned that Colin and Siobhán were not an "item" but were some species of cousin, long-established companions of the road.

I went to the castle earlier than Colin had suggested. When I passed through the square I saw that they were already laying the lunch out. They had the custom of setting out a couple of stout board tables in front of the refectory every day and covering them with breakfast, lunch, and dinner in turn, come one come all. The "refectory" was a solid Tudor-style building with an active chimney, where food was prepared for the town dwellers. There was a window of opportunity for breakfast and for lunch, and we would stop by, before work or during a break, sit on the benches and enjoy a repast with whoever else happened to be eating at the time. Dinner was a more formal affair; we all ate together. The people who prepared the meal ... I supposed they could be called servants, but only in the sense that all of us were servants. We did whatever task came to hand, but some were specialists and kept to their customary roles.

I had been kept busy, not overly, at a variety of tasks that first week. There was plenty of odds-and-ends work to be done, and I was happy to pitch in. The Dragons were by no means self-sufficient — they moved around far too much to keep a farm — but they had a fairly extensive garden outside the castle wall that needed to be tilled and weeded and pruned. The lawn up by the sun bower needed to be mowed, the intricate system of trails needed to be cleared of growing weeds and fallen branches. We gathered nuts and berries. Some of us shot rabbits. The seasons brought other tasks, gathering and splitting wood, butchering deer, clearing and turning the garden for the next year.

I worried about my wardrobe at first. I'd only brought one pair of jeans and it took a muddy beating. The laundress took care of it. A couple of buildings over from the refectory there stood a laundry with wide open doors and clothes strung on lines to dry, inside and out. There was plenty of water in the Dragons' fiefdom. In addition to their two wells, a little pond fed into a stream that carried past the town wall into the world beyond. In days gone by they washed clothes in the stream, but environmental concerns (others' not theirs) had caused them to discontinue the practice. Evidence of human pollution downstream might have brought regulators to their door. So the water had to be brought to the laundry in buckets. That was one of my tasks, and it made me feel less guilty about handing off my laundry for someone else to clean.

I passed the attractive ploughman's lunch laid out in front of the refectory and walked out of the town, up the path and under the portcullis into the courtyard. Arthur was there, seated in his yellow plastic car, looking about him in contentment, with neither the need nor desire to do anything else. It was a beautiful day, dry and sunny. I remember looking up at the blue sky as I walked between high walls, up the turning path to the Castle. I remember wondering as I walked, what Miss Widdershins could possibly want with me.

2.

Someone must have been watching for me. As soon as I entered the courtyard, Miss Widdershins came to her cottage door. It was an old-fashioned half-door, half opened, and she just snugly fit over the lower half. She swung it fully open and beckoned to me as she walked across the yard.

"We'll talk in the keep," she said.

When her son saw her, he rose inside his plastic car and started lifting it and slamming it against the stones while making a peculiar roaring sound.

"Yes, dear." She waved to him and continued on her way.

I followed her through the low arched doorway and into the keep. I got a quick impression: unfinished stone walls, an unused fireplace, lots of book cases, bleary windows with diamond-pattern panes and a big round table holding the center of the floor. Mr. Dinan was there ahead of us, the old-style lawyer, the little man with the big nose and grey pony-tail.

"It's such a nice day, we'll talk upstairs," said Miss Widdershins. "You can leave the book," she added, to his obvious relief. A massive open codex stood out on the table. I surmised that this must be the Black Book of Leuven, the fabled Book of the Lion that Con Gone-Away had died to hold. I was honored, and a bit worried, by the attention. What could they want with me, and with a lawyer too? Were they arranging a match with Cornelia? No, that would surely be for the Cats to do. But what if they were? Would I object?

We rose to the second floor by means of a spiral staircase

set against the wall, made of stacked pie-slices of stone, which rose simply though a hole in the ceiling and continued to the floor above. The second floor was open, without glass in the windows. More than once during our interview, a sparrow flew into the room, hopped about and flew out again.

When we were all seated at the second-floor table, a smaller version of the one below, Miss Widdershins began.

"I promised you an explanation of our long absence from New York," she said. "It has to do with our break with the Geese, or I should say the change in our relations with the Geese. I forget how much of our history I told you. It is relevant to our current situation. It is always relevant. You know that we came to the continent as exiles, all of us, the Dragons, the Geese, and the Cats. The Cats from Scotland, the Geese and Dragons from Ireland. Most intended to return some day, but it was not to be. Fortune had turned her back on us. I think we Dragons knew from the beginning that there would be no return. Exile is never a surprise to us. We are raised and trained to it.

"We had lived among the Gaels in Ireland and we sailed among them and remained among them overseas. Some knew our history, our descent from the Great King and our origin in the Isle of the Mighty. It was not so remarkable or unusual at that time; many of the families could claim descent from the great figures of the past, from Conn or Eoghan, from Ith or Ir, Eibhear or Eremon. But we alone kept our kingdom together unbroken, one generation to the next. It is our destiny.

"After the fall of the great French monarchy and the shuddering of the old order throughout Europe, those few who wished to retain their independence and who had picked up a taste for the roving life, took us as their leaders. They were wise. We alone had legitimate authority, whole and unquestioned. Such a life as they wished to live, to remain a secret nation among other nations, to remember and to vivify the past, is only possible under the aegis of authority and that could only be found with us. It is a hard life. A sweet life, the only life for those who love it, but hard."

The lawyer Dinan spoke.

"The King of the Dragons did not have direct authority over the Cats and the Geese. Technically he was their overking, *brenhin*. The concept was not new to us, but part of our history. They owed us tribute, military service, various visitation rights, judgement of disputes. Within those rather mild constraints, they governed themselves as they saw fit. The Geese were organized as a regiment, with the leader elected as Colonel and the various subordinate officers at his command. He is still elected, though he seems now always to come from the same one or two families. The Cats coalesced as sort of a makeshift clan under a new chief. They chose the greatest man among them as their leader, a Macpherson of high blood. That is why the name was put on them 'Cats.' From Clan Chattan, do you see?"

I didn't, but I asked Cornelia about it later. It seems the Macphersons used to be reckoned part of a larger confederation, Clan Chattan, Children of the Cats.

"That's why I'm Parsons," she said. "Same as Macpherson."

"The authority of the Dragons was remote, but real," Mr. Dinan continued. "Very real and very necessary. Most of the faithful, among both the Cats and the Geese, you see, were from the humbler classes. This made them all the more willing and able to accept the Pendragon as their leader, and made it easier to avoid competing claims. It was really a fascinating time, like a new foundation. What happened then, what we did, what they did. It reminds one of the accounts of the founding of city states and tribes in the early times, all over the world. A new beginning after a new flood."

Miss Widdershins said, "There was many a fracture, many a dispute and rebellion that was avoided by an appeal to the King. So much so that the position of the Pendragon, that is, the King, grew stronger over the years."

"And tribute was paid, from the beginning," said Dinan. "On that the record and the memory is clear."

"Even if it sometimes took an amusing form." Miss Widdershins laughed. "I remember when I was a little girl, we still got an owl every year at Christmas time."

"Birds of prey are fully traditional payments," said Dinan.

"I can still hear my mother complaining, 'What are we supposed to DO with all these owls?' They always seemed to arrive at the most inopportune times. We kept them outside in a specially constructed hutch. I made pets of them or tried to. I was disappointed when they stopped coming. They actually served us very well, keeping the rodents and the rabbits away from our garden. Their children still hunt these woods."

Miss Widdershins' attention was distracted. Arthur had

hauled his bulky form up the spiral staircase and had entered the room.

"Arthur! You know I don't like you to come up those winding stairs by yourself."

"*Bouff!*" Arthur dismissed her concerns.

"There's no railing..." she muttered. "All right you can stay, but you have to promise to stay very quiet."

"I promise."

He seated himself in a high-backed chair against the wall and spent the rest of the interview alternately sitting and watching us, and standing on the chair looking out the window.

Miss Widdershins resumed.

"The problem began with my brother, with the death of my little brother. His name was Arthur too. He should have been king. In the normal course of things, he would have been king. But he died, when still very young, in the hospital. We never should have sent him there. He was so young. I will never set foot in a hospital, whatever happens. After poor dear Arthur died, it fell to me to carry on. When my father passed, I became queen. But that proved hard for the Geese to accept."

Dinan explained, "The Geese are working from a different understanding of sovereignty. By their way of doing things, that is by the customary Gaelic way of doing things, in the absence of a direct male heir the king should be chosen from the close family, what they call the *derbfine*. Some cousin or nephew or even an uncle in rare cases. That was never our way. With us, the sovereign is always a direct descendant. We have been fortunate so.

There were two previous occasions when the sovereignty passed through the daughter; this was the third. Arthur's daughter carried on the line in old times..."

"He had no living son and in any case it could hardly have been carried on by Mordred."

"...and again when we were living in the North Country among the Gaels of Albany, the line was carried through the female child. That too occasioned something of a split."

"We lived in Scotland for some time," explained Miss Widdershins. "Well north of Dun Breatann. We kept the Vikings off the Margin of the Gael. Well, we helped, at any rate. But then things began to get too organized, too tidy and law-bound; too many great men with pretensions arose, and we moved again."

"So, as I say, when the Lady first took her place as queen, the Geese objected." Dinan would not be diverted from the topic. "It was so from the beginning, though they were pacified for a while. Their talk even stirred some of our own Dragons against us."

"Of course their discontent may have had something to do with the fact that the strongest claimant according to their law was MacOwen's second cousin. I have always believed that it did. An insipid man. He would not have made a king."

After a pause, Miss Widdershins continued the tale.

"After the Con Gone-Away fiasco, we at last had it out. That debacle provided their excuse. Or, to be more charitable, from their point of view it was perhaps the last straw. You know they helped us out of that situation, but it undermined their trust in us. They had come to see our relationship as a liability. Perhaps they had become so comfortable in this country they forgot the hidden costs of independence, of maintaining integrity."

"The meeting took place far from here, in the south. Only a few came from each group. The Cats were there. MacOwen and of course Stokowski and a few of his closest advisers and kinsmen. Cathal Maol, the pretender, was not there. A touch of *politesse* on their part but also a sign that the question of succession had become moot. I was there with Thomas — we were not yet married — Mr. Dinan here and Mr. Dillon, our modern lawyer whom you may have seen in New York, and some other of my advisers. Only a few councilors, in a room not much bigger than this. It was to me a sad gathering. It was plain that the Geese had already made their decision. Discussion only centered around terms."

"They had no grounding for a claim," said Dinan. "The book was unassailable. Our point was made and the succession was secured. Unfortunately, the Geese had moved beyond the legal question. They had come to believe that proper consideration of their own safety required a break with us."

"It was only a marriage of convenience," Miss Widdershins said. "It had not lasted so long, a scant two hundred years. We parted friends and for that I give great credit to the efforts of our lawyers on both sides."

"The disposition of all sides was amicable." Mr. Dinan deflected credit from himself.

"Our relationship with the Geese now is as *primus inter pares*. But no tribute, no rights of levy, no judgment of disputes. In time, we will drift apart — amicably still, I hope and expect —

but the trust, the certainty is gone. We have lost a great deal from the split. The strength of their arms, the intelligence to which they have access from their positions throughout the military and police departments, their help in navigating the ways of government, banking, business, travel. For years we have relied on them for passports, birth certificates, anything and everything with the stamp of the state on it. We have lost a great deal. But they have lost more although they don't know it yet. With our passing, sovereignty no longer dwells among them. There is no proper established authority they can look to, and that is the great need of a nation. They will decline into a club, a fraternal order at best, a criminal conspiracy at worst. They will not even know what they have lost when it is gone. It is very sad, although they did well to keep together as long and as faithfully as they did. It was really a remarkable feat. They never had the reason that we did."

She fell silent and was distracted for a while by Arthur standing on his chair, looking out over his kingdom, talking to the birds. Then she started, as if remembering something.

"The Cats stayed with us," she said.

She ran a finger over the dark pitted table wood, drawing designs known only to her. She spoke again.

"And that is why we have avoided New York. Our initial departure was required by the unpleasantness in the park. It was hard to know what the police would find, left by Gone-Away or by our own carelessness, so it was imperative that we leave at once. Afterwards, when things quieted down and the danger appeared to recede, the split with the Geese occurred and we found ourselves without our network, without the insight into police and government that we once had. It took us a long while to right the ship, to work out new systems of navigation so to speak. We have only started moving back to our old haunts very recently. It will be a long while before we can breathe easy again. It will never be as it was."

3.

They were finished, or so it seemed. I was amazed that they had told me so much, I who was nothing but an occasional guest.

"You asked no questions." Mr. Dinan smiled at me. "Do you understand this?"

"Yes, I think I do." There was one minor question which had been nibbling at me for some time, and I decided to ask it so as not to disappoint him. "Those people who moved into the Big House in New York after that whole thing in the park. Who were they? Were they Geese?"

"Yes," said Miss Widdershins. "We hadn't yet split at that point. But it wouldn't have mattered if we had. We still cooperate, they would still do that much for us. The Big House remains ours, of course. The other one, the one around the corner, we sold."

They had not yet made a move to rise from the table. Arthur came to Miss Widdershins' side and leaned his head against her over the arm of her chair. She mussed his hair and patted his head in absent-minded fashion.

"All the problems we alluded to," said Mr. Dinan, "and by that I mean the problems of navigating the rules of the state without tripping any alarms, have become much more difficult lately. This would have been true even if we hadn't broken with the Geese. The level of surveillance, the acceptance by the people of oversight, of constant oversight..." his voice trailed off. "The fundamental relationship between the individual and the state is changing in ways that it is difficult to predict."

I nodded.

"We can't rely on the old ways, on the old accommodations. We will need to keep abreast as the law changes."

I nodded again. Miss Widdershins was still ruffling Arthur's hair but was looking at me.

"Do you have any interest in the law?" Mr. Dinan asked.

"I don't know. I suppose so, in a general way. People are always telling me I should go to law school."

"If you were interested, and if you were interested in becoming our solicitor particularly, we could finance your legal education. Our current, what we call new style lawyer, is a Mr. Dillon whom I understand you may have met. A very competent man. But he will need help now and a successor later."

"That's very generous."

"The drawback, if one considers it a drawback, would be that we would make exclusive demands on your services. That is, you would exclusively be solicitor for the Dragons. That is not so unusual. Many great families or large organizations have lawyers that serve in similar arrangements."

"I wouldn't consider that a drawback."

"We could promise you a great variety of puzzles," said Miss

Widdershins. "You would not grow bored. New problems every day."

"I don't think I would be bored."

Mr. Dinan waved his hand as if he were a conjuror making a handkerchief disappear in his hand.

"We merely broach the subject today. No decisions need be made for some time, by either of us. But I am glad to see that you do not dismiss the idea out of hand."

Miss Widdershins rose. We were finished.

I liked the idea from the start, I confess. So much so that I put on the mental brakes so as not to be swept up in it. Lawyer for the family, like a mob lawyer, like Tom Hagen. It satisfied my need for romance, for the out-of-the-ordinary, the need that normal people make do without satisfying. It would solve quite a number of my problems. But I resolved to be deliberate. And God knows I wasn't anxious for three more years of school.

When I walked back down the narrow way and stepped out from under the lower gate, I looked out on the little town before me, that changeless little fairy tale kingdom, and I saw it in a new way. Perhaps I could help these people, I thought. Perhaps I could be their protector, their champion against an enemy they did not know.

I heard a hammer banging, like a blacksmith's, bending metal in one of the huts. I saw smoke leaking out a chimney. Something like fear took hold of me. It looked perfect and perfectly balanced, but for one raised where I had been raised it was impossible not to feel that everything that met my eye was somehow wrong. It was all unauthorized. There were permissions not given, forms not filled, inspections not made. There must be endless unmet regulations before me, for materials used in construction, for minimum standards of housing, for food preparation, waste disposal, fire safety, employment, use of non-commercial property. Even the pony might pose a problem. I shrank within myself, though I showed no outward sign, from the blow that I felt would come, that must come. If I learned the law, I thought again, perhaps I could help these people, help soften the blow.

Or perhaps it would not matter. By staying in place, the Dragons were drifting further and further away from the socially-mediated telecommunicating world outside, where even my father was finding it harder to function, where the virtual mob was always in session, where accusation was proof, where unsanctioned opinion led to irresistible ruin, and where the right people could always bring down the wrong people with the complaisant masses as their happy executioners. What could a lawyer do against that?

When I passed the tables, they had been cleared, but one of the servants saw me and called to me and they brought me out some warm cheese and warm beer, and a fistful of brown bread. I sat and I ate. This would all pass away, I thought, perhaps soon, but not yet, not yet.

5 Gracious Living

1.

The Cats' encampment was very different from Dragon Town. Up the leaf-shrouded lane, it was not as far from the road as I thought it would be, but well hidden. I visited it first the day after the meeting with Miss Widdershins in the Dragon's keep. I'd received an invitation for dinner and the Cats sent a driver, a man I didn't know, in mutton-chop whiskers. The distance was beyond easy walking, maybe four miles, maybe a little less. On my way over, I thought about renting a bicycle so I could visit Cornelia more easily. Without a phone connection, there'd be no way for me to check ahead to see if she was at the camp, and it could be a long walk wasted. On a bicycle, it wouldn't matter so much.

I looked at the trees on either side as we drove up the lane. The woods were thick, with a lot of undergrowth near the road's opening, but they did not have that heavy, immemorial fairy-tale quality I felt in the Dragon's forest. It was not so isolated either. When I climbed out of the station wagon, I could see through the trees a couple of low white houses for ordinary people.

Cornelia came out to greet me, striding through the ruts and grass of the campground in high boots.

"James! Welcome, welcome. At last you come to our camp. Let me show you around."

She took my arm like a pal, and started walking me around the place. There were ten, maybe a dozen trailers or recreational vehicles lined up around a clearing and a few big free-standing four-square tents. There were no permanent dwellings. As I looked closer, I saw that many of the trailers were hand-painted, most had awnings and some had window boxes, which combined to give them a festive appearance. I was surprised to see that some of the trailers were connected to fairly elaborate electrical and plumbing hookups that sprouted from the ground like mushrooms, as one might see in a commercial RV park. It was obvious that the Cats had not simply stopped in a random field; I learned later that the property was owned and managed by the Dragons, and provided a convenient summer base for those Cats who wanted to stay close by. The piece-de-resistance was a wooden hut, exactly like a hut one would find at a lakeside or scenic rest stop, that provided showering and washing facilities for those that needed them.

Toward the end of our circuit, I heard a sudden scuttling through the underbrush and a popping of twigs, distant but rapidly approaching until a voice called it off. Cornelia gazed darkly through the trees at the white houses I'd noticed on the way in.

"Them and their damn dogs," she said. "You can always hear them fighting over there, and they're always coming over here. It's getting so you can't go outside without a stick."

Then, brightening, "Speaking of animals, I have a surprise for you." We had arrived back at her trailer which was the one closest to the road, on the left, the first one we had passed. It was one of the larger dwellings and would need a separate tractor to get it moving. A portable flight of wooden steps stood in front of the door; above the door I saw a full moon and scattering of many-pointed stars painted against a dark blue and milky back-ground. All around the door and across the lower edge of the trailer there sported comical big-nosed people with long-brimmed green caps, emerging from leafy vegetation and dancing between trees, like a manuscript illumination executed by a cartoonist. Cornelia's work, I was sure of it.

She leaned across the wooden steps and scratched at the door. Then she climbed the lower steps and opened the trailer. As soon as she did, a grey cat ran out and wound itself around her legs.

"Remember?" she said. She lifted the cat and turned to me. "It's the kitten from the old days when we first met."

"I remember. I was hoping they'd brought it to you."

Cornelia laid the cat down and it ran off a few paces.

"She was just a kitten then. She's quite middle-aged and crotchety now."

"Eh? What's that?" Mrs. Parsons had appeared in the door-way.

"I was talking about the cat, Mama."

"Ah. Well, come in, come in. Welcome to our home."

I had observed the Dragons, and the others as well, upon en-tering a home liked to say something like, "God be with all here," but I wasn't quite ready for that yet. It felt forced. So I followed Mrs. Parsons in silence, with Cornelia behind me.

It was not a large space, but cunningly arranged. The win-dows were all propped open and there was a fan blowing length-wise down the galley. I heard a bubbling to the left and the scent of spiced cooking awakened my senses.

"Mama's cooking stew," Cornelia said. "An old traveler's recipe."

"Cornelia made the stew earlier. I'm just heating it up and putting it over rice."

They walked me past the kitchen area and showed me the one private room in the back where Mrs. Parsons slept. (Cornelia made do with a fold-out couch bed in the living area.) I noticed a keyboard sitting on Mrs. Parsons' bed, a few octaves wide, but with no legs and very little in the way of a sound box. It was a pretty thing, though, decorated with polished wood inlay.

"That's Mama's harpsichord. She's very good."

"Och."

"Play something, Mama."

"I have to keep an eye to the stew."

"Just a passage."

Mrs. Parsons groaned, though she did not seem displeased, picked the 'harpsichord' off the bed, and placed it on an open tray that folded out from the wall. Without further ado, she sat her plump person on the bed and began to play.

I was astonished. Cornelia smiled proudly at me and waggled her eyebrows. The little harpsichord tinkled quietly along and Mrs. Parsons played at stately pace the opening movement of an elegant baroque piece. She finished, then stood up.

"Well, I'd better get back to the pot."

"That was terrific," I said. "What was that?"

"Did you like it? I'm so glad. It was by Rameau; I forget the precise name of the piece. It's around here somewhere."

She climbed on top of her bed and, kneeling on the mattress, opened one of a series of cabinets mounted on the wall above the headboard. It was packed top to bottom with CDs. She shuffled through them until she found the one she wanted, then turned, scuttled on her knees off the bed and brought it to me.

"I am very fond of Rameau. I understand that mountebank Rousseau tried to discredit him. It was ever thus. Here, this one," she pointed to one of the titles listed on the back.

I looked at it, then with growing curiosity at her.

"You don't have the sheet music?"

"Oh, no. I can read music, I have some sheet music about the place, but not this particular piece."

"How did you learn it?"

"Oh, just picked it up. By listening. I don't suppose it's note for note with the record but close enough for my purposes."

"That's amazing."

"Och."

Cornelia nudged me and nodded, as if to say, "That's my mama."

"I'd better get back to the pot. You may wish to wait outside the pair of you. It's getting hot in here. Perhaps I should have cooked outside."

"It does get hot here, even under the trees." Cornelia said. "That's one of the reasons I want to live in a house one day, like back in Queens. Mama likes to travel, but I've had enough of it."

"I do, I do. But the road's no good any more. It's too hard to find a living. We'll all have to make a way to settle down."

"That's fine with me," said Cornelia.

"Right now, though, you'll just have to give me some room. Cornelia bring out the table, there's a dear."

We set a card table and some chairs before the steps and waited. Cornelia lit a lantern hung outside the door which emitted a smoke and an odor that were reputed to drive away bugs.

We didn't wait long. Mrs. Parsons nudged the door open with her rear end and carried a tray out to the steps, where Cornelia relieved her of it. There were three bowls of stew over white rice, a heavy-crusted loaf of bread, and half a dozen bottles of IPA. Mrs. Parsons uttered a short grace, unintelligible to me, and we tucked in. The dish was heavily spiced. There were tastes and scents I didn't expect. If I'd been served blind I might have thought it was Indian.

I complimented the food.

"Cornelia's doing. An old traveler recipe."

The bread was torn by hand and used to sop up the juices.

Cornelia pointed out the rising moon.

"It's full. They say it was full yesterday, but I can't see the difference."

She put her head back and gave a little mock howl.

"What on earth are you doing girl?"

"Howling at the moon."

"Whatever for?"

"It is a tradition among werewolves. They turn at the full moon."

Mrs. Parsons raised her eyebrows.

"Actually, I've heard that that's not a part of genuine werewolf lore," I said. "Some guy just made it up for a movie back in the 30s and it stuck."

"That's very disappointing," Cornelia said. "I'm not sure I can accept that."

"Why is it disappointing?" asked her mother.

"I like to think of werewolves changing at the full moon. It seems right. It makes me happy."

"You wouldn't be so happy if you saw a wolf coming after you."

Cornelia took a pin from her hair, which, now I noticed it, was arranged over her scalp in an intricate series of crossing braids.

"Silver," she said. "I am forearmed."

"A fat lot of good that pin would do you against a wolf."

I had the feeling that the trailer had witnessed many such conversations between the two of them over the years. I didn't have the heart to tell Cornelia that I thought the silver bullet motif might have come from the same movie.

After we were finished with our meal and we'd cleaned and stowed the dishes, we came out again and took our places by a fire pit where some of the other Cats were roasting potatoes and chops and whatever else they had with them. Mrs. Parsons brought forth a little hexagonal squeezebox and drew out some slow tunes, while humming with closed eyes. The man who had driven me over, with the mutton chops, scraped along on a fiddle and another man joined on a mandolin. When they played a song, the others sang along or took the chorus, as the moon moved above us through the darkening sky. I looked at the contented, weathered faces around the fire — most were Mrs. Parsons' age or older — and at their hair and clothes, an interesting combination, bits of color and finery, gold chains and silken vests, laid over tough durable garments made to last. If I'd seen them in another context I wouldn't have known what to make of them, but they welcomed me by their fire and it felt like home.

They brought me back late to my own front door.

2.

That visit convinced me that Cornelia was content with the Dragono-Cattic rules of propriety that saw to it that we always met within some social context, surrounded by family and friends. I shouldn't have been surprised — they were her rules too, the rules she'd been brought up with, and she hadn't been subjected to years of financially-motivated propaganda urging her to rebel against them. They had rebellion enough on their hands keeping to their ways in a hostile world; they didn't need to invent internal conflicts. I settled comfortably into the routine. In a way it made things easier between us, like the steps of a well-known dance.

I still didn't know how long I would be staying. I made use of the Dragons' delivery service to send letters home. They folded my letter in with the rest and within a few days it found its way to my parents' home. I learned from my sister that the little girl knocked and handed the letter to whoever answered. She was very shy and still ran all the way back to the car. Her name was Fiona. My family addressed letters to the Cats' post office box and the Cats would give them to me whenever we happened to meet, every few days. However often we met, it wasn't unusual for me to get two letters at once from my mother.

I was beginning to get to know the grounds. The Dragons had lived there so long that there were ruins scattered throughout the woods. Not far from the castle, though quite invisible through the thick dark trees, stood a ruined chapel, without door or window, with most of the roof gone and ferns growing on the floor. It was a relic of the days when a priest would stop and say Mass when he passed through on his rounds. The days gone by, when there were few priests for the territory and few schools for the children, and no grid to be on or off. I liked to sit in the chapel on the edge of the old sanctuary and look up at the waving trees through a gap in the roof. The altar and statuary had long since been removed.

The Dragons and Cats were still church-goers for the most part. They attended the nearest churches with the most convenient Masses. By design, they did not all attend the same Mass. "No one wants to see fifty of us showing up at once," Cornelia said. The church I went to, when I hitched a ride with the Dragons, seemed to be of the sort I categorized as a "vacation church." The sort of church my family would run into on summer vacation, still with the felt and guitars, very seventies, very soothing, very affirming, very American. There were no hard sayings to be feared.

Our own church back in Queens, St. Stanislaus, had experienced something of a rebirth. The new pastor was an actual Pole, from Poland, young, strong, effortlessly — even unconsciously — charismatic, who never got the memo that all that Catholic stuff, all that Mary and the saints, was no longer quite The Thing. The Polish element in the congregation was energized, and my mother was delighted. She even dared to hope that they might bring the Latin Mass back, now that Sixteen had thrown wide the door.

One day, when I had returned from my woodland ramble by means of a narrow footpath that may actually have been a game trail, I came up under the castle wall near a postern gate I'd never noticed before. The door was unlocked so I entered and wound up a narrow flight of unlit stairs. It brought me into the bright court-yard right next to the keep, where I found a little knot of people gathered before me. They were the three from the old days, Cornelia, Miss Widdershins and True Thomas, and they greeted me like a long lost friend.

"There he is," said Cornelia.

"The very man," said her uncle.

Cornelia approached me with a tied packet of letters in her hand.

"One from your sister, one from your mother."

I put them in my back pocket.

"I'm glad you turned up," said Miss Widdershins. "We were looking for you. I wonder if I could impose upon you and Cornelia to take Arthur to the park. There's a little park in town — Balin will drive you — where mothers are accustomed to gather with their children in the afternoon. It contains a playground as well, with swings and bars and various other equipage. We have no children here for Arthur to play with and it's important for him to spend time with other little people."

"You should have seen him the first time we took him," said Thomas. "O brave new world that has such creatures in it!"

"Unfortunately, I do not get along with the other mothers and nannies. I find their conversation to be tedious, frequently incomprehensible and sometimes obscene. They in turn do not like me. This makes things difficult for Arthur. Perhaps if you and Cornelia were to take him, he could mingle more easily with the other children."

I readily agreed. As Thomas went into the cottage to fetch his son, Miss Widdershins addressed Cornelia and me confidentially.

"One other thing I would request," she said. "Try to keep Arthur away from sticks. It alarms the other mothers. That's how he plays, you see, with my husband. Always at the fencing. It's harmless, but the others don't understand. Presumably they play sports instead."

Just then Arthur burst out of the front door, disengaging himself from nurse Dolores' hand, and ran at Cornelia, coming to a stop only when he plowed headfirst into her legs. She was his favorite.

"Oof," said Cornelia. *"Ciamar ça va, a veggar beg?"*

I'd been picking up a smattering of their language during my stay with them, but it wasn't easy. I'd never come across anything like it before. It was an amalgam — a shifting amalgam — of other languages, Gaelic strongly predominating. Not only were there different dialects between the tribes, with the Dragon's lingo being the most "mixed," but personal style also played a big role in their speech. Cornelia, for instance, liked to use a lot of French.

When she was younger she even tried to popularize personal end-
ings for English verbs ("thou speakest"), but only her Uncle Tom
even pretended to play along with that nonsense. It was like a code
spoken between old friends, heavily allusive, relying on remembered turns of phrase, and you had to be on your toes to keep up.
If a linguist ever got hold of the language, it might have made his
career, or brought him to despair.

Cornelia's greeting to Arthur, as she explained on the ride to
the park, meant, "How's it going, little boy?" a mixture of Gaelic,
French and Dragon talk.

"*A veggar beg,* that's Dragon talk. *Beggar* is their word for
boy, I don't know why. *Beggars and gannets,* boys and girls."

Arthur was happy to climb into the car with us. Balin picked
us up in front of the guard house in a long low well-preserved
old Thunderbird with a rumbling motor. Cornelia and I sat in the
back and Arthur bounced up and down on the seat between us. A
family outing.

3.

I wouldn't exactly say the visit to the park was a success,
though Arthur seemed to enjoy himself. We walked through the
gate, Cornelia and I, with Arthur between us, holding each of us
by the hand. Balin stayed outside, leaning on his car and smoking.
There were a number of children already playing on and around
the "equipage," the swings and the monkey bars, and a few plow-
ing up a big sandbox. Arthur broke from us and ran towards them,
then pulled up, uncertain of what to do. I had no experience in-

troducing children to one another, and thought it would be best to let Arthur to work it out himself. He was soon sitting in a corner of the sandbox, but none of the other children was disposed to lend him their toys, so he sat and drew Newgrange patterns with a twig. He seemed to be content.

Seeing him alongside the other children, I was surprised at what a hardy block of a child he seemed. The others in the sandbox looked fragile beside him. That might put some of the other mothers off, if they were silly. I also surprised myself with the reflection that the other mothers and nannies and caregivers might even find my Cornelia a bit intimidating. In addition to her unusual height and strapping physique, she sported what I was beginning to think of as the Cat style of attire, which seemed to owe a lot to the gypsies. She wore a long patterned skirt over high-heeled black boots, and a red vest over a long-sleeved ruffly white blouse. Her great spring of hair emerged from a knotted bandana used as a scrunchy. A pair of pendulous earrings completed the picture. The foreign is no longer foreign along much of the east coast of the United States, but I think Cornelia must have seemed genuinely alien to the baggie shorts and t-shirt crew. Too, somewhere in the recesses of their psyches, much as they would have been loath to acknowledge it, there probably still lurked stories of gypsies stealing children. I was glad Balin had stayed by the car.

I have no idea what they thought of me.

When I observed to Cornelia that Arthur was not playing with the other kids, Cornelia said, "Kids that age never play with each other. They just play *around* each other. He's fine."

All of us guardians hovered and watched our charges, oc-
casionally passing a word. After a while Arthur decamped and
asked to be placed in a swing. We took turns pushing. When he
wanted to swing himself we sat on a nearby bench and talked.

"What's a jed?" Cornelia asked.

"I don't know."

"It's spelled g-e-d. I think I need one to get into college."

"Oh GED, yeah, that's General Equivalency Diploma or
something like that. Yeah, that might do the trick. If you take the
SATs too."

"I say I was home schooled and take a GED."

"Do you really want to go to college? I don't think you'd like
it."

"I'm perfectly sure I'd hate it."

"Then why go?"

"My mother's worried. She's worried about the future. Things
are changing."

I nodded.

"Desperate times call for desperate measures, I guess. Still…"

"He wants to get down," Cornelia said, and laughed, for Arthur had wrenched his torso around to face us, while kicking his
feet.

When we let him down, he ran out of the fenced playground
and into the nearby trees. Sure enough, he hadn't been there long
before he returned dragging a dead branch behind him. He began
trotting toward the other children, bent on friendly roughhousing.
We intercepted him. For the first time he showed stubbornness.

We had to prize the stick from his hand, and he protested loudly, certain of the justice of his cause.

"The grip on this kid," I said.

"He's like an orangutang."

It was harder to soothe him than to remove the stick from his grasp. At length he gave in, and trotted back out to the trees, which wasn't at all what we'd hoped for when we came to the park. Kids in general seem to roughhouse a lot less than they did in my father's day though I guess they are more likely to take formal classes in self-defense.

"The nastiest kids wouldn't have anything to do with wrestling," my father observed once, reminiscing about his own youth, "while the nicest kids were always beating the crap out of each other. Maybe it has to do with a willingness to lose."

At length, Balin made his appearance.

"Time to go?" he suggested.

We got Arthur back into the car without fuss, though he did insist on retrieving and bringing back the stick we'd taken away from him. We didn't know if Miss Widdershin's strictures on the other mothers' conversation were fair, since we never exchanged but a few words between us.

4.

Arthur wasn't the only one who spent a good deal of that summer fencing. Once he saw I was Cornelia's friend, he became comfortable enough with me to include me in his stick play. He carried around a short smooth length of cylindrical stick with taped-up handle, like an abbreviated stick ball bat, and he would initiate merry attacks against my legs from time to time. His father saw me parrying one day, and something about my form arrested his attention.

"You fence!" he said.

It was true. Stirred by memories from Miss Widdershins' backyard, I'd taken up fencing at college. It was a lesson, a school even, in humility. I was quite good at the drills, the conventional exercises that teach the handling of the weapon. But what I learned there did not translate when it came to facing an active opponent. I was disappointed at how bad I was at the bouting. People told me I was 'overthinking.' They always say that about me, though it is seldom true. My problem is almost the opposite. When I act, I need to act without reflection. It simply takes me an inordinately long time to put my action together with my training. This chronic problem was compounded by the atmosphere of the bouts, the buzzer hookups, the milling spectators, the bewildering sequence of contests, the auditory and visual confusion.

I persisted. There is something peculiarly frustrating about being a bad fencer. The constant touching and buzzing, points scored against you without knowing how or why. The seemingly simultaneous touches — always called for your opponent. The advice, friendly and otherwise. I consoled my wounded vanity by telling myself that Olympic fencing is just a sport, a game, that it has nothing to do with 'real' fencing. Still, I had to acknowledge, a touch is a touch. You can't argue with that. But I persisted, and by junior and especially senior years, I had improved. I was putting them together, theory and practice, and I became a useful part of a winning team. Then I graduated.

"Would you like to learn something of our swordsmanship?"

I would indeed. So began a fascinating journey, all too short. I found that Dragon fencing, and Cat fencing, for Thomas was a Cat by birth, was within certain parameters, as idiosyncratic and personal as their speech.

Thomas taught without curriculum, figuring our way as we went along. I don't know whether he had ever taught anyone before. It was like play, really, but always with the serious end in mind. They had a great variety of wooden practice weapons scattered throughout the castle grounds, many of them in a couple of free-standing lockers set against the curtain wall. As we jumped from one weapon to another, each matched with its appropriate, often stiflingly hot, protective garb, I began to perceive certain constant principles in the Sword Master's teaching.

We spent a lot of time with two-handed swords to start with, although Thomas said they are the hardest to master. He said it was to make the universal problems of swordsmanship clear. It was not at all what I had expected, big swings like a baseball bat or a sledge hammer. Instead, the hands were held apart, and that way the swords could be manipulated very quickly and precisely, especially the light wooden practice swords. We went easy; even with padding and a helmet to protect us, they were dangerous. The thrust is a big part of two-handed swordplay the way Thomas practiced it — another surprise — and the wooden swords had a length of soft rubber affixed to the end to blunt the impact. It looked ridiculous, but it was necessary.

However formally we started, we very quickly found ourselves tangled up, at grappling distance. That was the first lesson.

"With swords, especially two-handers, if you're not careful you end up wrestling. Look at the old sword manuals the Germans used to draw. Half the techniques bring in wrestling, tripping, and throws. It's all distance. That's what sword fighting comes down to; all fighting, really. Keeping distance. The hardest thing to do. If you get close — when you do get close — remember your whole sword is a weapon, not just the blade."

Balin passed by frequently, and watched us with a certain amount of skepticism. He liked to address his comments to me, rather than to Thomas directly.

"That's in case someone goes for you with a two-handed sword next time you're in town," he explained. "Very practical."

Still, he would sometimes join us. I found it instructive to watch him and Thomas fighting. I saw how fast and decisive Thomas really was. I started to understand the movements by which distance was kept and closed. Thomas was the better swordsman, that was clear, but when it came to wrestling, I think Balin was the stronger.

Thomas' favorite weapon was the single-edge broadsword, the backsword, such as I had seen him use against Con Gone-Away. We practice with wooden single-sticks, with our hands protected by sliding wicker baskets.

"It wasn't so very long ago that the English used to have single-stick instructors and gymnasia in every town. That all died in the 20th century. But they kept the art alive for a long time."

This was a little more like what I was used to from the sabre, though not much. We kept the footwork narrower than I'd learned in college, with more attention to defense and recovery, since for what we were, in theory, preparing, anything close to a double touch was a defeat.

"Don't depend too much on parries," Thomas said. "I'm not a big believer in parries. That's one of the reasons I wanted to learn the Spanish style. Learn the parries, by all means, but in the heat of combat, when you might face a thrust or a cut from any angle, it's easy to miss. You're better to rely on distance, timing and body positioning. A parry is a last resort. It means something has gone wrong."

He reminded me too, "You can use your off-hand for the broad sword, when you're close enough and the time is right, though a lot of people like to keep their off-hand pinned behind them. That's one of my weaknesses, I've been told, using my off-hand too much," and he showed me the long trench carved into the back of his left forearm, an old scar. Seven years old, I would say, though I didn't ask him.

Arthur was often an interested spectator. Sometimes he got underfoot, but usually he kept clear. When he got carried away on a tide of martial valor, he would grab his wrapped stick and charge about the place thwacking at walls and branches, and chasing squirrels through the brush like a little dog. Thomas did not teach him, only played with him.

"Too young for schooling," he explained. "He needs to learn

his own natural motion."

A few times, Miss Widdershins even came out to do a bit of fencing. She employed what I once would have called "normal" weapons, foil and epee, which called for a little less in the way of padding. Arthur would laugh with delight when she appeared accoutered for combat, cry "Mommy!" and charge over, barreling into her and almost knocking her off balance. Again, rather like a little dog.

Miss Widdershins was very cunning and surprisingly quick, but cautious. Even with the Olympic weapons she adhered to Thomas' philosophy that treated the bout as a shadow duel and so avoided deadly risk. Trained as I was in contemporary fencing technique, I could often surprise her, though I always felt diffident when it came to poking her.

I remember on one occasion she asked me, "There, that technique, that parry. What was that? I never saw that before."

"I think they call that a Counter 5."

"Show me."

And when I had, and she had run through it a few times, she said, "Good. Don't use that on Thomas. I want to surprise him with it."

On occasions Thomas trained me with live steel, and though we went slow it was a thrill I have not forgotten. Mostly from that period I remember the heat and the sweat, the tired legs, the fun and the feeling that I was learning a living tradition of swordsmanship — a stream separate from any other, meandering through its own hidden woodland — and learning from people who had used the art to defend their lives, and still did on occasion. It was a thing, a craft, an art possessed by no other people in the world and practiced with no thought of money or accolades. It was Our Thing.

6. Cats and Dogs

1.

August passed. I spent a lot of time in the sun, weeding the garden, picking fruit, killing bugs, gathering produce for dinner. I spent a few days helping the others mow the meadow around the sun bower, swinging a scythe and gathering the fallen grass. I was always glad for a day's rain or an afternoon's downpour, to take the time to doze and listen to the heavy drops. Not to exaggerate; they didn't work me all that hard. But it wasn't the life I was used to.

There were always festivals to break up the monotony. On August eve they lit a bunch of big fires up at the sun bower, and the Cats came over for music and dancing. There were games, too, foot-racing, rock tossing, and every kind of fencing, where hard knocks were given and received. Thomas won whatever fencing contest he chose to enter, and Balin tossed his rocks the furthest. That was the first time, oddly enough, that it occurred to me to wonder what had happened to Balan, his twin brother, who had been his inseparable companion when I knew them up in Queens. I was going to ask Cornelia about it, but forgot before I got the opportunity. As the youngest male there, I actually did pretty well in in the foot race, second place. (I was Troll's "Distant Third" no more.) I was surprised and a little disappointed that Cornelia did not run, since I suspected she was quite speedy. She said she was saving her strength for the dancing. The athletic contests ended with a tug of war that almost everyone participated in, hauling on a rope as thick as a tree limb. Then we repaired, all of us tired and most of us sore, to the feasting.

Towards the end of August, I was surprised to see that the royal family were preparing for a move, and more surprised when I learned that the move was only to be a few miles, to the Cats' encampment. It was apparently a tradition for the king or queen to make a circuit among the neighboring client states — a custom which honored both those dispensing and those accepting hospitality — and no one was going to be put off by the fact that they only lived a few miles from each other and saw each other almost every day. The Cats prepared for the visit with great excitement, and I helped them do it.

They prepared the finest of the trailers, parked next to Cornelia's, which had a great boulder standing in front of it probably set down by a glacier in the long ago. The walls within were wood-paneled and smelled of cedar. If you woke up inside, you'd never know you were in a trailer; you'd just think you were in a tiny, tiny house. Mrs. Parsons took the lead in preparing for the guests' arrival. I remembered that the Cats did have a chief somewhere — I'd seen his children Donald and Mary at the gathering in Queens — but he wasn't living with them at this campground and Mrs. Parsons appeared to be the person of highest standing in his absence. She sang to herself *sotto voce* as we hung tapestries about the bedroom and I recalled that, apart from the excitement of a royal visit, it was her own brother and nephew for whom she was preparing. Cornelia painted a gold crown over the doorway, teetering sideways off a ladder with one hand flat on the outer wall. They sent me off to the hillside with a sickle and bag to cut wild lavender, and I couldn't help but think of the song as I gathered it.

> *Lavender's blue, dilly dilly, lavender's green*
> *When I am king, dilly dilly, you shall be queen*

The preparations were modest, and were completed in a few days. Mrs. Parsons had just put on the finishing touches, setting an unlabeled bottle of amber whiskey on the kitchen table with two heavy glasses, when word came that our guests were arriving.

They came in procession, just a few of them. I think it had been arranged for Arthur's benefit. Cornelia had brokered the morning's hire of three horses from Woodland Rambles Horse Farm. Miss Widdershins and Thomas rode these the few miles from Dragon Town with Cornelia leading, followed by Arthur in a tiny cart hitched to his pony, and Balin walking alongside. A handful of retainers walked behind them.

Cornelia came posting up the lane ahead of time to let us know they were about to arrive and a small crowd was waiting by the time they turned in from the road. Arthur was in a great state of excitement. He had a little whip in his hand which he waved around in token of greeting without, fortunately, touching the inoffensive little pony before him. Cornelia had tied up her horse and come over to join us. Even though he had been riding alongside her for the last hour, Arthur picked her out of the crowd. When they stopped, he climbed out of the cart and ran over to her in his usual puppy dog fashion, his friendly giantess.

"Hey, look here!" said Cornelia. "It's Old Guthrie!" which seemed like an odd thing to say. She told me later it was a Dragon term for the heir apparent, *An Goorthery,* "the Expected One," and it was also kind of a pun because we had all been expecting his arrival.

Then she bent over to pick him up, lifting from the legs.

"Oof. You're getting so heavy. What do you eat, rocks? Do you eat rocks?"

"Rocks," said Arthur. "Stone soup."

She tried to get him settled on her hip and he threw his arms around her shoulders. Miss Widdershins slipped easily off her horse and Thomas got off like a movie cowboy, swinging his right leg over his horse's stooping head. There was water for the horses and food and drink for the walkers as they were received into the campground. A couple of Cats had strung a scarlet banner from two long poles, and when they leaned them apart the banner spread and revealed a golden figure applied to the cloth.

Arthur turned in Cornelia's arms and pointed.

"The Dragon!"

He was just old enough, I thought, that he would remember this little family outing for a long time. I hope he does.

2.

With the move, the center of gravity of our little world shifted to the Cats' camp. Anyone who had business to bring to the Queen had to come to the royal trailer. There was no lack of visitors; as I had seen back in Queens, running the kingdom was a full-time job. Over at Dragon Town things slowed down. Some of the townsfolk, those who had processed with Arthur, were already missing, and a few others took the opportunity to go on road trips of their own. Those who were left still had to manage the grounds, but with fewer people needing to be fed, and especially with Miss Widdershins' somewhat fussy eye elsewhere, we took it easy. Even Dolores got a break; she did not accompany Arthur on the circuit.

In Dolores' absence, Mrs. Parson seemed to take on the role of nursemaid, especially when Cornelia was off at the stables. Thomas was in high spirits back among his own people, and could be found most evenings holding forth by the fire, arguing the minutiae of history or martial technique. Balin stayed in a nearby tent. I think he barely noticed the change. I learned that he had succeeded to the position of Champion after Thomas who was no longer eligible to hold it as the Queen's consort and The Expected One's guardian.

With so much traffic between the two camps, I found it easy to catch a ride back and forth. I was spending more and more time over at the Cats', sometimes when Cornelia was there, sometimes not.

On one occasion, Cornelia had just come back from Woodland Rambles, driven by our friend with the mutton chops, Mattie Donald by name. She climbed into the trailer and retreated to Mrs. Parson's room to change out of her stable clothes, while I stood up on the steps at the trailer's open doorway to pass some idle chatter.

I felt an unknown force approaching and turned to see Miss Widdershins marching toward me in what can only be described as high dudgeon. Inspired by the Cats' proximity to the park, she had renewed efforts to bring Arthur there to play with the other children. Apparently it had not gone well.

So rarely was she angry that her obvious rage was quite alarming. She got to the point without preamble.

"Who the devil is Madeleine Trotter?"

Madeleine Trotter, as some might remember, was a character in a musical children's puppet show that played on television some years back, a loveable but formally-spoken and somewhat overly genteel character. I understood immediately, as clearly as if I had been there, that someone at the park had compared Miss Widdershins to said character, and she had overheard it.

As I turned from the door I caught sight of Cornelia frozen in the hall, just emerging from the bedroom, eyes bulging, caught up in what I knew would be an irresistible tide of mirth.

"Don't let her in here," she managed to say before turning and running for the bedroom, closing the door behind her.

I turned to face Miss Widdershins.

"Who the devil is Madeleine Trotter?"

"Oh, she's a, she's a character from a children's show. She's a puppet."

"She is a pig, is she not?"

"Well, she's a puppet, she's sort of pink with long hair and..."

"Is she or is she not a pig?"

"Kind of a...a cartoon pig..."

"Och!"

Miss Widdershins turned on her heel.

I saw her husband waiting for her across the clearing. I saw that fear had at last entered his proud heart. I saw that Arthur was oblivious. He was stirring the ashes of the fire pit with a stick. I joined Cornelia inside the trailer.

I knocked on the bedroom door.

"Is she gone?"

"Yes."

"Come in."

When I opened the door I saw Cornelia roll off the pillow and start wiping tears from her face,

"I feel so disloyal," she said.

She sat up and swung her legs over the side of the bed.

"Poor Aunt Vivien. I shouldn't laugh. She's the kindest, noblest, most beautiful person know. But still, Madeleine Trotter. And she speaks French too!" for Madeleine Trotter the character was known for sprinkling her conversation with Gallicisms.

She buried her face in her hands and laughed some more. When she recovered, she said, "It must be those dimwits down at the park. They can't understand someone like Aunt Vivien. She is beyond their ken. So they react the way they do. It must have been very unpleasant. I wonder if Uncle Thomas was there."

"What do you think they will do ... he will do?"

"Do? Oh, nothing. It's just Bellymen talking. Ordinarily she wouldn't pay any attention to them at all. It's just that she's trying to find playmates for Arthur. I don't imagine she'll go back now, or send us back."

"Too bad. I liked going to the park."

"Me too. I wonder … I think some of the people who go to that park are the dirtbags who live in the white houses over there. With the dogs. Is 'dirtbags' right?"

"Dirtbags is correct."

"That would be bad. It's bad to have trouble with your neighbors. Trouble, trouble."

I heard a sound behind me and turned to see Mrs. Parsons. With narrowed eyes, she was the very picture of a suspicious Scottish woman.

"You two," she said. She did not like to see us alone in the trailer.

"Mama, you missed the fireworks. Did you see Aunt Vivien?"

"She seemed displeased."

"Let me fill you in…" and she did, though she had to explain 'Madeleine Trotter.' Mrs. Parsons listened but did not smile.

"Well, I think it's all very silly," she said when Cornelia had finished. "And you're very silly too."

Cornelia said nothing, but looked smug. She knew she was right.

3.

It was during this period that Colin returned from his Midwest circuit. Siobhán did not return with him. I was glad to see him and I think he was glad to see me. We spent a good deal of time together, sitting at the table in front of the refectory, drinking beer from tankards while he smoke a long pipe, feeding the dog and chatting with whoever stopped and stayed. A pleasant way to spend an afternoon or morning; I felt like a figure in a Dutch painting.

In addition to his abilities as a huckster and an artisan, Colin was a skilled handyman who did piecework all about the surrounding area. When the time came to hit the road and start scrounging up work again, he gathered his tools, loaded his truck and extended an invitation to me to come along. I thought it might be an interesting change from gardening, but wasn't sure if they could spare me. The informal foreman of garden and field was a sleepy heavy-set man whose name was apparently Garn. That's all anyone would tell me when I asked his name, so eventually I took to calling him Garn like everyone else.

"I suppose so," he said when I asked if they could spare me.

He added, "We'll let you know if we need you again later. You may be glad to come back to us. Have you ever done that kind of work, carpentry and the lot?"

"No. I did warn Colin."

"He'll teach you what you need to know." He thought for a moment then said, "Just wait a day till I run it by management. They take a special interest in you."

Word came back the next day, and the following morning I was off on the road with Colin. It soon became clear I had made an unwise decision. I had no experience with manual labor other than the bare minimum around our house, and I found it a grind, both the work itself and the long slog trying to scare up a job.

Colin was up for anything, though most of what we did had something to do with wood work or repair. That part of the country had to be traversed by automobile, not on foot. Colin would do the talking, knocking on doors while I waited in the car.

I was the "other guy," I decided. After we were finished, or so I imagined, a neighbor or relative would come by, see our work, and say, "Oh, you got finally got your back steps fixed."

"Yeah it was getting dangerous. It was a guy we've used before, the one I told you about. He comes round in a truck this time of year. He fixed the garage door too. There was another guy with him."

I was that other guy. I had no skills, did a lot of basic fetch and carry. And dig. I was kind of like an idiot nephew brought along to learn the ropes. The saving grace was Colin. He was patient in a way that suggested that he felt no temptation not to be. I finally put a name to that quality that I'd noticed back at the Renaissance festival. Humility. A lovely and uncommon quality that sheds a healing light over every situation.

Most of those who hired us were people whom Colin had worked for before, people who didn't worry too much about credentials or bonds, who were comfortable with informality and knew what they were getting when they hired us. On one occasion we contracted an especially big job, a good-sized backyard deck that had to be laid out with strings and levels and the lot. Colin called on three other men to help with the job (I think a couple of them may have been Geese), and I did a lot of holding things steady and digging holes.

During our lunch break, spread out over the grass, I could see the men were turning over a new piece of news, and some of them practically giggling.

Colin saw I had trouble following, so he said, "Big news about our Siobhán. She's expecting. That's a bit of a surprise, though our Siobhán, God bless her, was always a bit ..."

"Sprightly," suggested one of the other men.

"...sprightly."

I thought that she must have been younger than I gave her credit for, and then I heard the men saying with some excitement, "*Fanfaidh sí, fanfaidh sí,*" which I understood enough to know meant, "she's staying."

"She'll be staying with us, too, and not leaving," Colin said. "Not a doubt of it. I expect we'll be gathering for a wedding in the near future, *buíochas le Dia.*"

I asked Colin a question then that I'd been mulling over for some time.

"Why are there so few children among you?"

"Oh, we have a few, though not at this camp or at court. A few far and wide, throughout the country and the world. You see, many leave when they have a child. Some leave to get married, maybe they marry a Bellyman like your grandmother did, or maybe the pair of them leave together. They might stay till they have a baby and then they're afraid it will be too hard to raise and keep a child as a Dragon with the world turning the way it is. It's a bit easier for the others, who don't quite have our..."

"Splendid isolation," said the same man.

"...splendid isolation. Aren't there any *páistí* at the Cats' camp?"

"No."

"Hmmph. That's why it's a very big deal when a child is born among us, or when someone marries in. A very big deal, if you understand me."

At the Cats' camp they certainly made a big deal of Arthur, Mrs. Parsons, as I've said, playing a leading role. She would entertain him when Miss Widdershins was immersed in affairs of state. Her music fascinated him. It was from them I first heard *Griogal Cridhe, Beloved Gregor,* his favorite, a lament sung as a lullaby, *O ba ba mo leanbh* — "Bye lo my baby" so to speak — which ended, if I understand it correctly, with the dead love of the singer, her "sweet fragrant apple," lying with the back of his head on the ground. Arthur loved it for the beauty of the tune and was untroubled by the sadness of the lyric.

Children's music often contains some grim or otherwise 'inappropriate' things. They take no harm from it. Quite the contrary. My grandfather used to lull my father to sleep with an old British army song he learned in the service:

O it's whiskey whiskey whiskey
That makes you feel so frisky
In the corps, in the corps, in the quartermaster corps
Mine eyes are dim, I cannot see
I have not brought my specs with me.

4.

After the big deck project, the handyman work hit a welcome lull. I was glad of the opportunity to fade into the background. I didn't mind helping out now and again, but I sure didn't want it to become an expectation. I had come for a visit, not for a job.

In early September I'd had the happy idea of starting riding lessons at Cornelia's stable. I could always find someone to drive me at least part of the way there from Dragon Town. It took a bit of figuring to mesh our schedules, but we could usually arrange it so that once or twice a week I hit the trail in a little group of riders led by Cornelia. She took her duties seriously, always pulling back to correct and encourage the riders, and the horses. She thought it would be fun to pretend we didn't know each other, so I was just one of the group. She was a good instructor.

After we finished our rides, Cornelia would go back to the barn with the horses and I'd usually walk back to the Cats' camp. It wasn't far; there was a footpath (also used by the horses in parts) which cut out half the distance traversed by the long looping paved auto road. It was a pleasant walk, running alongside a sylvan stream for a while. It brought me back to the road only a couple of hundred feet from the entry to the Cats' camp.

On one memorable afternoon, after just such a ride, when I entered the Cats' camp stepping out from the leaf-covered lane, I saw Miss Widdershins standing by the big broken boulder that stood in front of her trailer, holding Arthur by the hand as he balanced on the rock. A peaceful scene, I thought.

I knew Cornelia would get off work in a half-hour or so, and

I wanted to wait for her. I'd noticed a short distance up the main road a raspberry bush dotted with fruit, so I knocked on Cornelia's trailer and bummed a plastic container from Mrs. Parsons. It was my thought to pass the time picking raspberries. When I came out of the trailer and turned back toward the road I saw that Miss Widdershins had Arthur by both hands and was singing to him while he did a four-year-old's dance:

> *Killiecrankie is my song*
> *Sing and dance it all day long*
> *From my elbow to my wrist*
> *Now we do the double twist*

I picked raspberries and plunked them into the container for a good long while, hoping to see Cornelia coming down the road, back from the stable. Time passed, and at length I concluded that she must have been picked up by someone and driven off on some errand I didn't know about. I had enough berries anyway, they were beginning to mush together at the bottom of the container. I headed back to camp.

I was nearly out of the lane when I heard a horrid sound. Four clawed feet over the ground, the depraved snarl of an attacking dog, and Miss Widdershins screaming, "Thomas, Thomas."

I dropped the raspberries and ran to the clearing. I saw Miss Widdershins holding Arthur high in the air, whirling round and snatching him away from the jaws of a white dog, leaping and snapping, round and round.

The dog swung wide and lost his angle of attack, then gathered himself and made ready for another attempt. By that time,

Thomas had burst out the door of his trailer and jumped down the stairs. When the roaring dog charged again, he was ready for him. For a fraction of an instant I thought I saw him move out of the way, but he had shifted his feet for a cleaner path of action and perhaps to open a way to lure the dog past him. When the dog went for Arthur this time, Thomas collapsed on its body as it passed, pinning it to the earth. It turned its head to snap at this new enemy, but Thomas grabbed its two hind legs and sprang to his feet, as quick as ever a fencer recovered from a lunge.

Now he turned, and swung the dog once against the broken boulder, then again. The first impact knocked him stiff and the second killed him. Thomas dropped the dog at his feet.

A man came running through the woods, shouting.

"What did you do to my dog?"

Thomas bent, lifted the animal by its collar and tail, and handed him to the man.

"You killed my dog. Why the — did you kill my dog?"

"He went for my son."

Thomas spoke as if it was a great weariness to answer the man.

"You didn't have to kill him. I would have taken him."

"Do you know what a dog like that can do to a child?"

The man was holding the limp body of his pet by the collar now, and letting it droop on the ground. For a moment I thought I saw the man reach behind him, as if perhaps he had a weapon tucked into his waistband. He might have had a gun concealed there; he was wearing a denim jacket over a tank top. But he saw

Balin coming up fast through the trees, and Mattie Donald the mutton-chop man appearing in a doorway behind him, and who knows, maybe even me approaching from the other direction. Every second more Cats were appearing ready for battle, the women too.

He picked his dog up and slung it over his shoulder. I thought it was some kind of mixed-breed pit bull, short-haired with heavy jaws and an artificially muscled body.

"This isn't over," he said. "This is not over. You haven't heard the last of this. Trailer park freaks."

The further away he walked, the more threats he uttered.

Arthur had buried his face in his mother's safe warm bosom. He now pried himself free, looked after the departing pair and uttered his judgement.

"Bad dog."

The Cats had gathered round, Mrs. Parsons among them. They were mortified that the little prince had been placed in danger in their camp. Balin too was remorseful.

"I didn't hear him coming. I'm getting slow."

"He didn't make a sound until the last moment," said Miss Widdershins. "They train these dogs to their own destruction. Are you all right sweetheart?" to Arthur, brushing the hair from his face.

"Yes."

"What do you think about all that, what he said? Will he bring the police? Will he come back with friends?"

"He won't bring the police," Balin said. "He doesn't have a

leg to stand on. The dog was on our land. They probably get complaints about these dogs all the time. Besides, it's dollars to donuts he's a parolee, that type. He won't get the police involved."

"Think he'll come back in strength?"

"I doubt it. Who wants to die for a dog? Maybe later, something by guile, some shabby revenge."

"I think it's time to go back, me and Arthur. Back to *Dinas an Dragain*."

"O, don't go back like that," Mrs. Parsons protested.

"It's high time we be going back anyway. It's all right, Mary, your hospitality has been exemplary, as always. We are very grateful to you."

"I'd hate for you to go back like that."

"I think Arthur might feel better for a change of scene. I think I might too. That man upset me. I detected something unsound in him. And it really is time for us to be getting back."

They went round and round like this for a while, and while they were doing so, Cornelia came back. She saw the group milling about in an unfamiliar configuration, with Miss Widdershins and Arthur at the center. Even at the time, I was pleased that she came to me for an explanation.

"Those damn dogs. I told you," she said, when I had finished. "Are they OK? Is little Arthur OK?"

He seemed confused and a little scared, but more, I think, from the seriousness of the adults and the great fuss being made, than from memories of the dog. Cornelia went over and knelt down and cooed to him and he threw his arms around her neck.

Miss Widdershins had a happy inspiration. She and Arthur would go home, but Cornelia and I would go with them to keep him company. She calculated, correctly, that Mrs. Parsons would be mollified if Cornelia went along with them, as a representative of the Cats. Mattie Donald was sent to get the car, and he soon returned. The crowd parted to let him through.

When Arthur understood that we were driving back to Dragon Town, he protested.

"My pony! What about Fernando? He'll be lonely."

"We'll bring him over in a couple of days," said Miss Widdershins. "Perhaps you can come back and drive him home."

"I want to say goodbye."

So we waited while Arthur ran over and explained the situation to his horse, pulling his head close and earnestly addressing the large mild face. Fernando seemed to understand.

All objections answered, we climbed into the car, Miss Widdershins and the driver in front, Cornelia and I in the back with Arthur between us. It was an unceremonious departure, but he remembered to wave to the people on the way out. They saw us off with three cheers.

Arthur was quiet on the way home, but did not seem in low spirits. I thought he had recovered well from his fright. When we rolled into Dragon Town we stopped in front of the guard house and got out, three of the doors opening at once. I opened Miss Widdershins' door and stood aside to let her disembark. The woman of the house came out onto the porch, and called to us.

"Oh! Welcome back. We were not expecting you for a few

days."

Miss Widdershins waved, said, "There was a change in circumstance," and began walking towards the house.

I heard a short joyful yip and saw Fergus, the big grey shepherd, running towards us. He slowed and trotted toward Arthur, wagging his tail. Then he stopped. By some wisdom inherent to his kind, he felt and understood the fright and the danger that his little master had suffered. He whined in worried sympathy and stretched forward, licking Arthur's face.

Arthur hugged him and buried his face in the dog's thick fur. Then he straightened and pronounced a second judgement.

"Good dog."

7. Beg, Borrow or Steal

1.

The folks back at Dragon Town would have preferred a few days advance notice of the Queen's return. They'd let the place slide a bit, and had been counting on a grace period. But whatever tizzy they fell into was unnecessary and short-lived. If Miss Widdershins noticed anything amiss, she didn't mention it. She seemed abstracted; the royal eye was elsewhere. I think now that she may have had a premonition.

Thomas returned later that day, and the retinue came back the next, leading Fernando hitched to an empty cart. The people in the white houses did not see fit to bring the Case of the Murdered Dog before the authorities. Balin had judged rightly.

In truth, it was a fine time at Dragon Town. We had plenty to do, which kept me away from Colin's handyman work. We had to catch up on the mowing. I spent a brisk day and a half picking grapes in the tiny vineyard, which ran up a slope on the margin of the garden. The harvest was full on, and the fruit was falling out of the trees. After years of relying on supermarkets, I rediscovered what ripe fruit was like. All the garden plants were bowed under their own weight. The pickers were often stuffed full by the time they sat down at the lunch table. What we didn't grow was easily bought, cheap, ripe and in plenty. I realized it must be farm country outside the narrow network of roads I had traveled.

The bugs came on in force, a never-ending warfare. The Dragons had some kind of homemade spray they forced out of a hand-held dispenser that looked like a bicycle pump. It was somewhat effective, but by no means an impregnable barrier, and as soon as it wore off the bugs regrouped and attacked again. Garn said that if we had turkeys we could run them through the rows and they'd eat a lot of the bugs, but we had no livestock, so we had to fight them ourselves, often one by one.

As we entered fall, it turned to jacket weather around the evening fire. My wardrobe, which I'd worried about on my arrival — contained as it was within the compass of a single backpack — held up nicely because people were always giving me clothes. Pants, work shirts, a sweater, several hats, a silken vest from the Cats. The only things I had to buy for myself were underwear and a pair of boots, purchased at the Army-Navy store in town. My problem was going to be bringing all this stuff home with me when the time finally came to leave.

With the cooler weather came more frequent rains. Mud became a problem, and we laid down boards in strategic locations to work from and to walk over. I began to see the wisdom of carpeting Dragon Town in cobblestones. On one particular rainy day, when the water fell from sun-up to twilight, not hard but steady and cold, I was privileged to take part in a royal expedition to Emmeline's Sundry Store, the local general store and trading post.

It lay in the opposite direction from the town, the stables and the Cats' camp. In contrast to the shiny new markets I'd seen at the shopping center, it was self-consciously old-fashioned, with a raised board walkway running around two sides of a rambling shingle-sided building. Cars could park in the gravel in front or across a wide lawn that stretched to the right, tamped flat by many visitors. There were ceiling fans within, but no air conditioning.

There was something for everyone at Emmeline's. The natural configuration of the old building, with lots of wings and level changes, lent itself to an arrangement of merchandise by clearly defined sections. When you walked in you were in the standard tourist-oriented section, with heavy T-shirts, caps and sweats stenciled with the names of local towns and parks, along with coffee mugs, thermoses and an upright cooler stocked with energy drinks and lemonade. Further back, toward the cash register, the goods ran more to the outdoorsy, a tightly packed section of camping gear, tents, stoves, individually carved sticks, boots with mink oil, and knives under a glass case. Take a right, and you walked down a flight of two steps and found yourself in a new wing which was devoted to local products of all description — honey, preserves, cheese, handcrafts — and antiques, from dolls to old silver to a cast iron pump. Miss Widdershins and Arthur stepped down into this little kingdom.

Cornelia and I turned left, I following Cornelia, into a room that was like an old bookstore. I was very glad Cornelia had come along. With the court's move back to Dragon Town, it was no longer as easy as it once was to bum a ride to the stables, so it had become harder for me to schedule riding lessons. As a result, I had been seeing her less often. Cornelia was a great reader, favoring classic children's books, and knew exactly what she wanted. She collected the books of Joan Aiken, her Dido Twite series built on an alternate history, where the Stuarts held the throne and the schemes of the Hanoverian pretenders kept everyone on their toes. For my part, I never in my life read less than I did during those three months I spent up at Dragon Town. Maybe I needed a break after college; maybe there were too many other new things claiming my attention. In any case, there was no lack of intellectual stimulation at the town. Aside from learning their language, I could take advantage of a fortnightly lecture series given by Mr. Dinan, the lectures being on whatever subject happened to interest him or Miss Widdershins.

I wandered among the shelves, floor to ceiling most of them. I'd learned from Cornelia that when people finished reading they could bring their books back for a store credit, so it was half-library half-bookstore. Given the in and out traffic and given the fact that they probably didn't make much money from books, I was impressed by the neatness of the arrangement.

I was not surprised to come across a hefty occult section. Most of these were new age, mass-market paperbacks, but some of them, old hardcovers from the early twentieth century, were frankly manuals of witchcraft, complete with helpfully labeled drawings of pentangles to assist in the summoning of demons. I thought that this area of Pennsylvania must be like the Catskills, where my family vacations, with an old rural underlay, but close enough to the city to draw colonies of artists, health cultists, neo-pagans, latter-day transcendentalists, the whole crowd of the spiritually enlightened and those who cater to them.

I drifted out of the book room back into the central section and past the knife case. Miss Widdershins was standing just at the entrance of the local odds-and-ends section, with a wicker basket over her arm, looking through jars of honey. I saw Arthur approaching her from the opposite direction holding a puppet embraced in his arms, a pink puppet in a white satin dress with long golden hair. He held the puppet facing away from us, but I think I knew who she was even then.

"Well! What is that object?" said Miss Widdershins tolerantly.

Arthur turned the puppet and stretched it up towards her so she could better appreciate its glory. I saw the snout and the merry cheeks and the smiling pig face. It was Madeleine Trotter. This cleared up a minor mystery. Madeleine Trotter had been off television and out of the public's mind for a few years now, so I'd been surprised that the dirtbags in the park had remembered her well enough to summon her up as a term of abuse for Miss Widdershins. Of course they must have seen the puppet in the General Store, so their tiny minds had the image ready when needed.

Miss Widdershins was amused by the beaming creature.

"Isn't she a sweetheart?" she said. She received the proffered puppet into her hands and took a closer look. I saw her with the tag between her fingers, reading.

"Oh, no," she said. "Absolutely not."

She handed the puppet back to Arthur. He was stricken, amazed. He had not thought that anyone could resist this radiant object. It was plain he was in love.

"But Mommy!"

He showed it to her again. There must be some mistake.

"No, dear. We'll get you something else, just not this partic-ular puppet."

"Pleeease!"

The reality was setting in, that he and his lady love, so lately found, might be parted forever. He clutched her tighter.

"Pleeease."

"No, dear."

His father was standing nearby, but with no inclination to take part in this clash of wills. He gazed into the middle distance, as if trying to read a poster on the far wall.

Miss Widdershins moved towards the cash register, trailed by Arthur.

"Put it back, dear, we'll find you something else."

She placed her basket on the counter. Arthur dared greatly. He made no move to return Madeleine Trotter. Tears welled in his eyes. I reflected then that I had never seen him cry, or whine or beg. He was doing all three now.

"Pleeease, Mommy." He sat Madeleine on the counter next to the basket. "So beautiful."

Miss Widdershins sighed heavily. She bent her head and rest-ed it on Madeleine's own, and her silver threads among the gold mingled with the puppet's shiny locks.

At length she sighed again, raised her head, and looked at the counter-man with defeated eyes.

"How much for the pig?" she asked.

2.

It was just about a week after Madeleine Trotter joined us at Dragon Town, and I was sitting at one of the wooden tables drinking a long ale after lunch. The pale yellow leaves had begun to fall and tumble across the cobblestones and I'd already spent some peaceful mornings sweeping. The Queen liked the center of town and the courtyard to be neat. The garden pickings were getting slimmer. The focus of labor had lately switched to the harvesting of grapes for wine and apples for cider.

Colin came and sat beside me. At first I was afraid of a new job, but there was a certain unaccustomed — one might say confidential — orientation to his posture, sitting crossways on the bench, that suggested to me that something else might be up.

In his eyes was an unfamiliar expression. If I had to give it a name I might call it 'conspirator's glee.'

"James Ward. Would you be interested in a little *eachtra* tonight? An expedition?"

"Sure. What's up?"

"Justice. The collection of a bill. There's a guy — I did his driveway for him and he won't pay. Just the deposit. He came up with all sorts of excuses, tried to find problems in the work. I've seen it before. He can obviously pay; he has the money. It's never poor people who stiff you, unless they're *flat* broke. We did a quick job, which is what we charged for, just resurfacing. He knew that's what he was getting. That's why we only charge a third of what others charge. That's why people hire us. But he won't pay."

"So what are you going to do?"

"In such cases," said Colin, "I like to help myself to something of equal or lesser value. We're going to take our payment in goods. I happened to notice, while I was working there, that he has a junky old motorcycle chained up in a shed at the back of his property. You can't see it from the road. I'm going to take that motorcycle. I've got it worked out with Davy K. He's going to be waiting in a road behind the house with his van. We just have to get the bike to the van. I need someone to help me roll it. I don't know if it can start — I doubt it — and in any case I don't want to start it up in the yard. So I need you to help me roll it through the woods to Davy's van. There's a trail — it shouldn't be too hard. Are you game?"

It sounded kind of crazy, but I didn't have anything else to do that night, so I said I'd go. The whole thing reminded me a little of college.

"Excellent. I'll call you out around midnight."

He did a quick seated pivot on the bench, and was gone.

True to his word, he knocked on my door at the appointed hour. I'd dozed off, which surprised me. I was dressed and ready to go. Colin gave me a scarf, not for the cold but to muffle my face to discourage identification. Davy K. was waiting in an unmarked van, in front of the guard house. I knew him from work; he was the fellow with the ready quips.

As we drove out along the unlit roads, I reflected on my situation. It seemed that whenever I was with these people, I was drawn into a night time foray of some description. I was no longer a child, nor even a college student, both stages of life at which idiocies of this kind might be excused. Stealing a motorcycle might lead to trouble. Still, Colin seemed to know what he was doing.

We drove swiftly along deserted roads. I soon lost sense of direction. We drove in silence except for Colin's hissed whistling. He was obviously enjoying himself. We slowed to a stop without warning, tight by the side of the road, against what looked to be a solid barrier of woods. On the other side of the road, we were facing a blank space between two driveways, about fifty yards apart. No houses were in sight. Colin and Davy K. got out and I followed suit. Colin walked back up the road behind us, and found what he was looking for within a few paces: the trail into the woods. Davy K. opened the back door of the van and began pulling out a ramp.

"OK," said Colin. "Let's go."

He wrapped his scarf around his lower face and I wrapped myself in mine. There was still a three-quarter moon in the sky, so we had some light to travel by. I noticed the trail we were walking over. It was packed dirt without underbrush. There were a few exposed roots that might be a problem, but otherwise it seemed like a good path for us.

Colin stopped suddenly. We had reached the yard. The house before us was unlit. The trail gave out, and we had to push through some bushes for the last few feet; as we did so a security light sprang to life. Even here in the country, I thought.

"Fast."

Colin sprang forward. There was an open shed in the back of the yard, just a peaked roof over two walls. I saw the motorcycle within, an old-fashioned affair. It looked prewar — World War II. I saw that Colin had brought a long-handled bolt cutter with him, carried in a knapsack. He made two cuts, at the back and at the front, and I heard chains drop. I kept anxious eyes on the house. The light was plenty bright enough to waken a sound sleeper.

"Got it. Push!"

He took the handlebars, I bent myself to the seat. It was harder than I thought. We had to fight clear of the bushes first, and even on the trail it was hard to keep the wheels on the smooth dirt. I kept waiting for a shotgun blast behind us. More than once I had to lift heavy in order to help the back wheel over a root or out of a rut. It was an extra effort to get the thing back onto the road, but we managed, and Davy K. was waiting for us. Colin was giggling. He was a patient, humble man as I have said, but he did enjoy a good *eachtra*.

Davy K. helped us push the cycle up the ramp. We pulled up the ramp after us and pulled the doors closed behind it. Davy K. hurried around the front and started the van. Soon we were leaning around the country roads again. Colin and I unwrapped our faces. We stayed in the back with the motorcycle. It was a pretty thing for all it was so old.

Davy K. called back to us.

"I think we just passed your man on his way home."

"What?"

"On the road. I think we just passed each other. What's he doing out on the road at this hour? He should be home counting his money. He doesn't look honest to me."

"Do you think he recognized you?"

"God, no. I've got the hat pulled down and he never got any kind of look at me at all before anyway."

We kept going. We slowed, turned and I heard us rolling over leaves. When we stopped it was at an unfamiliar place. I got out and saw a shed standing in the middle of nowhere, attached to nothing.

"It's a safehouse," said Colin.

"More of a storage facility."

There was no fear of detection here, so they set up a lantern. We rolled the motorcycle back down the ramp, worked it into the crowded shed, covered it with a drop cloth and padlocked the door.

On the way home we all sat in the front and Colin sang. It was a long drive. I would never have been able to find my way back to the storage facility by myself. At length we turned into the old familiar driveway. Davy K. left us off in front of the blockhouse, then backed off and drove away. I never saw him around Dragon Town again. I think he may have been a Goose.

The whole affair had taken less than three hours, including travel. It had all gone very well, I thought.

3.

A few days later, I received another summons to appear before Miss Widdershins at the castle. This time, the summons was not delivered by Colin.

I had become accustomed to living at Dragon Town, so I did not bother my head speculating about the reason for this particular call. I'll find out when I get there, I thought. No one paid attention to me as I walked through town. They'd become accustomed to me too. Most everyone was out of doors, enjoying the fine autumn morning and the rustle and tick of leaves falling on stone.

When I stepped into the keep, I was surprised to find Colin there before me. I noticed that he had changed his appearance, clean-shaven and with a fresh buzz cut in place of his pony tail.

He started when he saw me enter.

"Uh oh."

We hadn't long to wait. Miss Widdershins entered a few moments after me, carrying a handful of newspapers, wearing her little gold-rimmed spectacles. She walked around to the far end of the table, and settled into an ornate high-backed chair.

"Sit, sit," she said, waving us into the empty chairs on our side of the table.

She got right down to brass tacks, addressing Colin.

"You have a fondness for vintage motorcycles, do you?"

"Oh, that. Yeah, let me explain…"

"Please do."

Colin laid it all out, the man's refusal to pay, his deafness to entreaties, Colin's resolve to obtain satisfaction.

"You see, it's my practice to take something of equal or lesser value as payment for my work."

"You place a high value on your labors."

"Eh?" Colin was nonplussed.

"According to the complaint filed with the police, the motorcycle is valued at $65,000."

"What?!" Colin half rose from his chair.

"Perhaps the man exaggerated."

"But it was just an old motorcycle. I thought it was just an old motorcycle."

"A valuable antique, apparently. The police are treating the theft with commensurate seriousness."

Colin was outraged, as if the man had perpetrated a fraud upon him.

"But why would he keep it out in the shed, just with a chain? Why wouldn't he lock it up in the garage?"

"I have no idea. Perhaps he was working on it. Perhaps he thought it was safely out of view. In any case, you may or may not be pleased to learn that he did have other security measures in place. Your exploit was partially captured by an automated camera. My source tells me the view is only partial. It is fortunate that you arrived and left by the back way, out of the camera's range. It is also fortunate that you were both swaddled as to the face. Nevertheless, he will clearly recognize you, Colin. As well, you have made yourself quite a figure in the neighborhood, with all the work you have been doing. It is therefore imperative that we get you out of the state *tout de suite*. We will arrange it. You've already taken a step in the right direction, I see," here she passed her hand over the crown of her head, indicating Colin's new military cut. "The vehicle. Is it in the Cage?"

"Yes."

"We'll return it. We'll leave it in a safe location and place a phone call to the police. So, Colin, prepare to travel. I'll have someone drive you out in a van or something. To North Carolina, I think. Occupy yourself with your craft. We'll bring your truck down to you later."

"I'm sorry for the trouble," said Colin. "I had no idea it would create such a problem."

"If we deal with it soon enough, I expect the problem will disappear. But really, you're going to have to learn to let such things go. It is not always necessary to claim satisfaction. Occasional loss is part of life. You should know this."

"You're right, you're right. I know. I also wanted to say that it was my idea, I sort of dragged James Ward into this…"

Miss Widdershins waved him to silence. I think — I am sure — I saw her struggle to banish a tiny incipient smile from her face.

"That is evident," she said. "Now, James. I appreciate your desire to go along with …with these lads, but we simply cannot have you involved in such scrapes. I understand that you did not work on this particular resurfacing job with Colin. Is that correct?"

"Yes."

"Nevertheless, you have been seen about with Colin, so any suspicion that falls on him would naturally adhere to you. That, coupled with the video footage of you actually committing the theft, makes it too dangerous for you to remain here. First, you should follow Colin's lead and change your appearance. A shave and a haircut should do it. Then we'll drive you back to New York in a few days. Don't take it too hard. We will be leaving for the south within the month anyway. Most of us don't spend winters up here."

I didn't know what to say, so I nodded.

"You will of course need to make your farewells to Cornelia and her mother. Now, I will have to make arrangements to shift you two and to return the motorcycle."

We both rose.

"But I would like one more word in private with James."

Colin executed a little bow and left. When the door closed Miss Widdershins spoke again.

"I want to make sure you understand: if you are still entertaining the idea of becoming our attorney in the future, it is doubly important that you avoid any taint of lawlessness now. Are you still entertaining that idea?"

"Yes, definitely."

"Then I'm afraid you cannot join these other more carefree types on such escapades. They can very easily get out of hand and cause lasting damage, to you and to others."

"Yes, I understand."

"The other thing I wanted to emphasize is that this is only a temporary separation. You are in no sense leaving in disgrace. We all expect to be on the road in a month. You'll just be leaving a few weeks early, for safety's sake. I'll send for you when I've worked out the traveling arrangements. In the meantime, gather your belongings so as to be ready to travel. And do be sure to come see me before you leave."

And with that, I was dismissed.

4.

I went out to the Cats the next day. I think Cornelia knew something was up the moment she saw me. I had shaved and gotten a close haircut (from the laundress who practiced quite a number of trades.) I think I looked like a person who was intending to return to developed lands.

"Your moustache! What happened to your moustache?" Cornelia asked when she opened the trailer door.

"Well, that's a bit of a story."

"Come in, come in."

Mrs. Parsons was sitting on the couch, Cornelia's bed in the evening, playing solitaire. She looked up from her cards as I entered; I could see that she too knew something was up.

It was a tough story to tell, but not as tough to tell to them as it would be to tell anyone else; my parents, for instance. The ethic propelling the action was not unfamiliar to them.

When I was finished, Cornelia said, "That Colin! I could strangle him."

"I thought he had more sense than that," said Mrs. Parsons.

"I didn't. So you have to leave now, immediately?"

"Within the next couple of days, I think. I am just waiting for the call."

"I so wanted to go on the Ride with you on All Hallows Eve. It's just a few days away. Colin!" and she flopped into a chair and folded her arms.

"There's always the May Ride next year."

As it happens, we were destined to miss that too, though we

didn't know it at the time.

"That's true."

"Your aunt says you'll all be moving south soon anyway."

"That's true. We break up camp for the winter. You don't want to be in one of these trailers through a Pennsylvania winter if you can help it. They get *cold.* It comes up right through the floor."

She was already getting over her disappointment and beginning to plan.

"I'm not sure where we'll be. There are a number of places. Sometimes we'll be on the road but I'm sure we'll settle somewhere. We can still receive letters from you if you leave them in your box. I'll talk to the Dragons. They'll pick them up if I ask them to. Your letters might take a while to reach me though. First they'll have to get to the Dragons and then to us. It's easy for me, I can just put a stamp on mine and mail them to you."

It was discouraging to be back to letter-writing again.

Mrs. Parsons had risen.

"I'm sorry you are leaving early but we are very lucky that you have been able to pay such a long visit. I hope you have enjoyed the summer as much as we have."

I assured her that I had and thanked her for their hospitality.

"And now I suppose you two will want to make your farewells."

We walked up the golden lane alone, on a carpet of fallen maple leaves. Since I'd learned that I would be leaving shortly, I'd had some time to reflect on my sojourn with the Dragons. It was something of a test, I thought, or not so much a test as a trial period, to see how we got along and whether I could live in their world. I thought we did well on both sides. The nonsense with the motorcycle was no impediment — quite the contrary.

It was difficult for me to gauge Cornelia's feelings on the matter. She seemed content with the stately pace of our developing relations. I was not one who could guess a girl's unspoken thoughts or intuit her hidden feelings. Anything she wanted me to understand would have to be written in block letters and stapled to my shirt front. All I could say is that we seemed very natural together, without any of the boom-and-bust cycle that others describe, the anxiety, the recriminations. I did sometimes wonder whether things were going as well as I imagined, when the line from the old song came back to me as a little nagging fear, "I lost my true lover for courting too slow."

"Do you remember this?"

Cornelia pulled from around her neck, forcing it past her hair with difficulty, a thin woven chain. She showed it to me and I saw that it was attached to half a gold ring, her part of the token that had been left in my mailbox.

"Do you still have yours?"

I pulled out my wallet. The ring had worn a raised semi-circle into the leather.

We set the halves together to make a full circle.

"Last time it was seven years separation. This time a few months."

We each replaced our halves, Cornelia ducking her head into the chain, and then we strolled down the lane arm in arm.

"You like it here, don't you? You like my family, and living with them."

"I do."

When we got to the end of the lane we turned around and walked back, while the autumn wind scattered gold around and over us. And so we made our farewells.

By the time we got back to Cornelia's trailer, there were Cats gathered at the entrance, whichever of them happened to be around at the time, and they all shook my hand and clapped my back and wished me the best. Mattie Donald had the car ready to drive me back. No one showed any great surprise. The Cats are used to sudden departures.

I got the call next morning. I had already gathered my belongings. Somehow, I was leaving with more baggage than I'd brought, even though I'd had to throw out some of my worn clothing. Before I left, I went up to the castle to take my official leave. Thomas met me at the courtyard gate. He held a notebook in his hand.

"Take this with you," he said. "It's something I worked on in the early days. My own version of a *Fechtbuch*. It's mostly pictures, but it might help you remember things over the winter."

Miss Widdershins was sitting in the central garden, surrounded by spent fruit trees, on a low stone bench with Arthur beside her. She was holding in her lap Madeleine Trotter, and the three of them were carrying on an animated conversation. She had no way of knowing how Madeleine Trotter really talks, and she gave her a Scottish burr. Arthur bounced with delight in his stone seat and from time to time placed a hand on the puppet's round cheek.

"Och, what are ye talkin' about you daft child?" said Madeleine Trotter, while Arthur laughed.

When they saw me, Miss Widdershins laid the puppet down and rose.

"James. I'm glad you stopped by. I hope you have a safe and easy trip home."

She reached under the bench and brought forth a jar.

"Please bring this home to your mother. It is clover honey. We have an interest in the hives; they're a little to the west of here. I see Thomas gave you his book to look at. I remember years ago seeing him working on it. It may be a little hard to decipher. Also," she reached under the bench again, "I know you are a Latinist, so please accept this with my compliments. It is an early edition of Horace. A pretty thing."

When I got the book home I discovered it was a rebound edition printed by Aldus Manutius, dated 1509. But for now, I merely accepted it and thanked her for both presents. She extended a hand, and I tucked the presents in the crook of my left arm, took her fingers briefly in my right hand and made a little bow. Arthur had risen from his seat and he too shook my hand with grave formality.

"Good bye," he said. "I hope you come back soon."

As I left, I heard behind me Madeleine Trotter taking up again the thread of her remarks. I would miss this place, I thought, as I walked down to the car I knew was waiting for me. The people, the stone paths, the heavy trees. But it was time to go for a while. It was time to go back to New York.

As I walked through the town square, those who saw me gave me a wave, then returned to their work. The Dragons too were accustomed to sudden departures.

8. Home Again, Home Again

1.

Mattheus drove me home. I knew him from the old days, the former "Army Jerry," that is, *armiger*, the Dragons' armorer. It was he who had driven Cornelia and me back from the driving range, after we'd followed Con Gone-Away to his lair seven years ago. It seemed that he was playing a major role in settling the Dragons back into their New York haunts and habits in the wake of their breakup with the Geese. Another guy rode with us. I didn't know him. He was a big dark fellow from somewhere out west. He didn't say much. The car was loaded with bits of business, mainly wrapped addressed packages, with some files, books, and even household items. It was a long, boring drive. I was very tired for some reason and drifted in and out of the intermittent conversation. As I got closer to home and started recognizing the roads and the landmarks, I perked up.

My house was the first stop. I collected my new belongings from the back seat and my pack from the trunk. I felt like a traveler fresh from the sea, returning after an absence of many years. No one expected me; I hadn't time to send a letter that would be sure to arrive before me. I stood on the front stoop and knocked, although I had a key in my pocket. I could imagine the bother inside such as always occurred when my parents heard an unexpected knock at the door. It was usually a nuisance, someone trying to persuade us to buy new windows (estimates were free!) or delivering a pizza at the wrong address. I thought belatedly to spare them annoyance and maybe a trip down the stairs, and I was fumbling in my pocket for the key when my mother opened the door.

"James!"

My mother was astonished, and, plain to see, relieved. I knew the letters I'd been sending her had allayed her fears somewhat, but nothing short of my actual tangible presence could convince her that I hadn't been spirited away for good.

She kept hold of me, by my arm or my shoulder, even when the others came down to greet me, as if to defeat any attempt by persons known, unknown or suspected to make me disappear again.

My father eyed me fondly.

"You look good," he said. "You've been spending a lot of time outdoors. All that yard work agrees with you."

My unforeseen advent was a big hit, but also a cause for some curiosity. My family was not used to sudden departures or arrivals.

"We didn't know you were coming," my father said. "Did you write? If you did, it hasn't reached us yet."

"No, it was pretty sudden. I didn't think the mail would arrive before me, so I didn't bother to write."

"What was the hurry? Anything happen up there?"

My mother looked at my father angrily, as if she was afraid his questions would disturb the good magic that had brought me home.

"What does it matter? He's here."

"No, nothing special," I said. "They tend to do things rapidly when they do them. They'll all be moving south for the winter soon themselves."

The suspicion surrounding my sudden appearance was general throughout the family; it lingered, palpable though thenceforth unspoken, throughout the winter. Almost the first thing my sister said to me when I got home was, "So … what did you do?"

"I didn't do nothing."

"You must have done something. Come on."

"It was only supposed to be a visit."

"Well … OK. But you're not fooling anyone."

I could hardly tell them that I'd stolen a motorcycle, so we let it lie. The only person innocent of suspicion was my grandfather. He knew I'd been away but had trouble remembering where or why.

"Now where were you again? At school?"

It interested me that, when I made my explanations, he did remember Miss Widdershins and Cornelia and the events of seven years ago perfectly well. It was only the more recent past that eluded him.

I soon learned that all was not well at the Ward household. After many years, decades even, my father had lost his job. His little publishing house had been bought by Hacker and Kopf, one of the giants, and in the process of consolidation, his position had been eliminated.

"I wasn't surprised. The position they'd jerry-rigged for me wasn't working. It didn't make sense. I'd tried to tell them that for years. They were trying to do two things at once and did neither well. They wanted to keep their traditional publishing model, but make it 'cutting edge.'" My father could not utter those two words without contempt, however mild, creeping into his voice. "My position fell between two stools."

"Couldn't they find something else for you to do?" said my mother. They must have had this conversation before but were reviewing it for my benefit. "Another position? After all these years."

"HK had their own people. If they have to choose, they're going to keep HK staff. I wasn't the only one."

My father took a sip of wine, which he made seem like a sort of rhetorical trick, a spacer.

"It's a good thing we have this house paid off and that you all have graduated," he said. "I don't expect to find a job very easily, not at my age and in my industry. And with my dearth of contacts. I never did learn to network. Right now, the only income we have is Dad's pension and social security. And that's enough."

"Hey, what about my salary?" my sister asked.

"That's yours. That's not household income."

"You put that in the bank," my mother said.

"No, I don't see any way around it," my father continued. "We've got to keep the old man alive."

We all looked at my grandfather hopefully. In the past he would have been good for a quip in riposte, but now it was plain he was barely following the conversation.

"Where do you work?" he asked my sister. "Out on the Island?"

"Yes. At Cholmondeley Day School. I teach music."

My grandfather smiled. "To all those rich kids out on the Island. I'm sorry my father didn't get to see that. He really would have gotten a kick out of it."

My father recounted his misfortune with his usual equanimity — and with even a sort of grim enjoyment at having the world prove as treacherous and irrational as he always said it was — but it must have been a heavy blow financially. When I brought up the Dragon's offer of law school tuition a few days later, it was in this context, as an unlooked-for boon, a heaven-sent money-saving opportunity.

I did not get the giddy reaction I'd hoped for from my parents.

"Do you *want* to go to law school?" my father asked, admittedly a natural question.

"I don't know. I've thought about it. It would give me something to do, a clear path."

"That's a big commitment, in time and intellectual energy, even if the money is taken care of. The world is full of miserable lawyers."

"That's true, but it might be a path worth exploring..."

"What do they expect from you in return?" asked my mother. "They're not just going to pay for law school out of the goodness of their hearts."

"Well, the thought is that I would apprentice as solicitor for the family."

"The Family." My mother folded her arms and nodded. "What kind of family needs a lawyer?"

"Every family needs a lawyer."

My mother clucked in impatience.

"What kind of family needs its own personal private lawyer?"

"Let me ask you something," said my father. "If you go to law school for a couple of years, and decide to chuck it, it's not for you, are you going to owe them any reimbursement? Or if you start working for them, then decide to move out to California and take a job there, or wherever, how are they going to take that? Do you have to work for them for a set number of years?"

"And how much will they pay you? And what law school would you go to? The whole thing is crazy."

I didn't know. I didn't know any of it. These were good points all, which hadn't occurred to me. It was the way of thinking out in Dragon Town, which I had adopted. When Miss Widdershins said something would be done, we all simply trusted that she would do it.

2.

There were other things amiss at the Ward household. My sister was seeing a young man of whom my father did not approve. He was a musician, a music student still but also a violinist with one of the local Long Island symphony orchestras. He considered himself, as I was told, an elevated personage and he was supercilious in a way that set my father's teeth on edge. I could see by the way my mother took pains to defend him that she didn't like him either.

I met him, and spent time with him at the dinner table. He would sometimes stop by and eat dinner with us before he and my sister took a train to attend a concert in the city. I really can't remember much about him. I guess I wasn't paying close attention; I just have a series of impressions that it's hard to piece together into a person. He was about my sister's size, kind of flabby in the way musicians often have, liked to laugh, reasonably polite to my mother. He did have a uniform condescending attitude that seemed to be partly based on his generation — same age as my sister, an age at which most Bellymen think they know everything — and partly on his function as a classical musician which brought with it the associated glamor of high culture.

He was openly contemptuous of traditional or folk music. When he heard that I played the bagpipe, he said, "I hope you're not planning to play anything for me," and I replied, "I wouldn't dream of it," and we were each satisfied with our dismissal of the other. Interestingly, he was also volubly contemptuous of para-classical music such as is found in the works of Rogers and Hammerstein, and even Gilbert and Sullivan. Yet he was a fan of some of the grossest, rankest rock bands who produced sound thoroughly scrubbed of anything beautiful, enjoyable or even identifiably musical.

When my father privately remarked on this apparent contradiction, I, who had observed this phenomenon in other snobs, advanced my theory that fear of mockery was the driving force behind these aesthetic 'judgements.' Aside from music that was officially stamped as high-culture or politically useful, the only music such a snob could allow himself to enjoy must possess no sentimentality or prettiness nor any positive quality that could be mocked by the hard nihilists who are our arbiters of the acceptable.

"Fear of mockery," my father repeated, and he nodded. "That whole generation … mockery rules their world. They've always got to be laughing at something. Everything's a joke, a take-off, a spoof. Like I said to Mr. Giggle-and-Sneer, everything's a parody with them."

In a moment of impatience with our guest — such moments were becoming more common with my father, and not just in interacting with my sister's suitor — my father had made this very observation to him directly, last time he was over for dinner. Jeffrey had reacted to the sight of a Christmas crèche, newly arranged on our mantelpiece, with a tag from *Life of Brian*.

"It is an unfortunate characteristic of your generation that you never experience culture or emotion or religion or even life unmediated by parody. You don't know what you're missing. "

I'm pretty sure Jeffrey disliked my father as much as he was disliked by him.

My father was still thinking about the incident a week later, perhaps a little ashamed that he had been goaded into open disapproval. I took the opportunity to introduce a topic which had been on my mind for some time.

"I wonder where parody would rank in Mr. Dinan's Six Stages of Aesthetic Experience," I said.

I'd been wanting to try out Mr. Dinan's theory on my father. He had expounded it at one of the courtyard lectures sponsored by Miss Widdershins. Most of those lectures were given by Mr.

Dinan, who was our resident polymath. His profession as an "old style" lawyer made him an expert on history, genealogy, literature, philosophy, music and even, apparently, horticulture. I think Miss Widdershins mainly arranged the lecture series for his benefit, to give him a chance to discuss ideas, answer questions, enlighten.

I remember the morning courtyard, listening to the "aesthetic experience" lecture, Miss Widdershins sitting straight in a straight-backed chair up front, with Thomas and, surprisingly, an awed and quiet Arthur at her side. The rest of us were strung out behind them, some in chairs, some on pillows or blankets. The regulars were there, those I thought of as the upper stratum, like Garn the steward and Mrs. Parsons, who attended most of the lectures, sometimes with Cornelia in tow. Cornelia was not at this particular talk. As well, there was a good scattering of townsmen and Cats and newly-arrived "through travelers" sitting in the rear, attracted by the topic, by the chance to gather in the warm open air, or simply by the change of pace. If they got bored or confused, they could always watch the birds, hopping, cheeping and flying across the yard.

Mr. Dinan stood at a portable wooden podium, and brought with him a sheaf of papers, his notes, which he consulted from time to time. He fielded questions, mostly from Miss Widdershins and Thomas, during and after the presentation. He was obviously enjoying himself. Though I missed many of the allusions, I found the topic interesting and tried to write down the main points as soon as I got back to my room. I felt it slipping away from me as I wrote, but I think I got the gist of it. I knew I would want to discuss it with my father and my grandfather, though now that I was home I thought it would be fruitless to try to explain it to the latter.

Mr. Dinan's interest was chiefly literature. His approach was not to look at works of literature as if they were produced in a factory and brought before an undifferentiated mass of people for consumption, but rather to "match up" types of works with the culture that — produced seems the wrong word — lived with them. I forget exactly the words he used.

"See, he thought different cultures at different stages are capable of understanding, or as he said 'receiving,' different kinds of works. He had a Latin tag that illustrated it: *Quodquod recipitur* ... whatever is received ... I forget exactly."

"That sounds familiar," said my father. "Hey, Dad." My grandfather had just started ascending the stairs, both of them creaking in concert. "Dad!"

My grandfather appeared in the doorway.

"Are you calling me?"

"Dad, what is that Latin tag, *Quodquod recipitur* ... whatever is received...?"

"*Quidquid recipitur ad modum recipientis recipitur,*" said my Grandfather without hesitation. "Whatever is received is received according to the mode, or manner, or condition of the recipient. It's a Scholastic principle. What made you think of that?"

"It's something the Dragons were talking about," I said. "Their theory of literature."

"Yes?" said my Grandfather. Then he smiled beatifically upon us and drifted out of the room. We heard him climbing the stairs again.

"Anyway, Mr. Dinan said that the First Stage of Aesthetic Experience takes place in an intact, traditional, mythic culture. He said that was the highest stage. Every rock, every stream, every family even has its own stories, its own legends attached to it. People move about through a sea of constantly occurring memories, allusions, tales, and songs, reviewing them in their own minds, recreating them, adding to them. Just living is 'living mythically'; everything public and private, human and natural, real and imagined is woven into one continually unwinding aesthetic tapestry. That is the highest stage of aesthetic experience according to him."

"The Second Stage of Aesthetic Experience occurs when the intact culture is on the verge of dissolution, whether because of … what did he say? … invasion, dispersion, perversion or conversion. I think that's right. Anyway, that's the time some great genius arises and synthesizes the whole dead or dying culture into a great work that immortalizes and memorializes it. He cited Homer and Malory as examples. He said that paradoxically, the second stage produces the greatest art, but not the greatest aesthetic experience. They argued about whether Dante should be included. Miss Widdershins said yes, Dinan said no. It all turned on whether or not 'the medieval synthesis' could be considered a traditional culture in the same way as the others."

"What did they decide?"

"They didn't. I think Miss Widdershins was mainly arguing

to show Mr. Dinan that we were interested. He also said that one of the unfortunate aspects of Gaelic literature was that it was definitively interrupted while still squarely in the First Stage, so that the great synthesizing genius never arose. They argued about that, too, but in the end they agreed that the Gaels went straight to the Third Stage."

"Ah," said my father. "The Third Stage."

"The Third Stage is when the original cohesive mythic culture has definitely fragmented, but people still depend on it, and its remnants form the basis of people's internal lives. That's when what he called the fragmentary geniuses arise, people who explore and elucidate certain limited aspects, 'fragments' of the tradition. He included the Greek dramatists, Aeschylus and Sophocles, Vergil, some guy named, I think, O'Reilly, and Cervantes. They argued about Cervantes."

"*He* might be an example of parody," said my father, "at least the first part of *Don Quixote*. But obviously he had a lot more going for him than mere parody. Maybe there's good parody and bad parody."

"I thought Aeschylus might actually belong to the first stage, but I didn't say anything."

"With all the interruptions and arguments, I'm surprised he got through his lecture."

"They didn't argue for long. Just raised a question or objection, then moved on. In the Fourth Stage, the original culture has fragmented further, there's a break between artist and audience. The artists can no longer assume that they inhabit a common world of belief and memory with their audience, and this state of affairs gives rise to what Dinan called the creative geniuses, who create new forms and almost new worlds to enchant the people and bring them back to themselves. He counted Shakespeare in this stage, I forget why. He insisted, by the way, that the listing of the stages in no way implied any denial of the inspiration, abilities or achievements of the later stage artists. It mostly related to the resources which people have available in themselves for experiencing art."

"It sounds like this Dinan has set himself an ambitious task."

"Oh, he's nothing if not ambitious. He's a pure intellectual, alone and with nothing and nobody to stop him."

"Sounds dangerous."

"In the Fifth Stage of Aesthetic Experience, there is no longer any moral, intellectual, metaphysical or mythical world that is held as real *either* by the artists *or* their audience. Even the authors have lost their unitary worldview at this point. Everyone is a *monad,* adrift, at sea, so the goal is only the realistic representation of this or that slice of life. That would be like realistic novels and plays, and movies too, I guess."

"Like modern novels. I wonder if he'd include people like Conrad."

"He might. As I can understand it, you *can* have a serious purpose in any one of the stages. You're just limited … you and your audience are limited in what they can expect from each other. One of his themes was that real artists were always, whether they knew it or not, trying to recapture through their art the original unified world of the First Stage."

"Now the Sixth Stage is when the possibilities of realism have been exhausted, it's boring and meaningless, and the only way you can entertain or reach people is with shock, like from the grotesque or violent or obscene. The Rhymer quoted Caliban, 'You have taught me language and my profit on't is I know how to curse.'"

"Who is The Rhymer?"

"Cornelia's Uncle Thomas."

"Why do you call him The Rhymer?"

Because he was chosen by the Queen of the Fairies.

"It's a nickname," I said. "I don't know why."

I continued, "I guess movies with a lot of special effects and violence would fit into this stage, though I don't think Mr. Dinan would have seen any of these. He didn't spend much time with Stage Six. He did say that it could sometimes — in what he called 'inverse artists' — be driven by a desire to annihilate all memory of the cohesive mythic world of the first stage."

"Maybe parody would be part of that," said my father. "At least some parody, not the creative kind, not like Cervantes. The kind of parody I object to, the really corrosive parody, seeks to replace or destroy the original. When it becomes ubiquitous it destroys the possibility of aesthetic experience entirely."

After a pause, he continued. "Some audience they have over there. I am surprised he could get so many people to sit still for all that."

"Oh, I don't think most of them knew what he was talking

about. They sat and listened as a courtesy to him and to Miss Widdershins. I suppose in a way, most of them are still holding at Stage One, if that's possible."

"That is the land of lost content, I see it shining plain, the happy highways where I went, and cannot come again," said my father.

Housman was one of my Grandfather's favorite poets, so my father knew him well. Perhaps he'd be a fourth stager?

3.

I easily slipped into my old way of doing things, which involved a lot of reading with my leg hooked over the arm of an easy chair and a lot of general layabout. The uncertainty about my future was still there, but this time it was certified, so to speak. I was waiting for a summons. I assumed the Dragons would call me out again in the spring, and I wanted to be ready to go. It was almost like a reverse school schedule, with me leaving home during the summer vacation, and coming back in the fall.

My parents were content to wait as I did, and the time passed swiftly; we were in the Christmas holidays almost before I'd fully unpacked and settled. There were some difficult explanations to be made to relatives during the yuletide visiting and hosting. My sister primed the pump by telling everyone I had joined a commune. I couldn't exactly deny it, but I tried to laugh about it. I didn't care to go into it deeply. There was no explanation I could give them that would have been understood, or even heard. *Quidquid recipitur* as Grandpa said.

My mother actually helped me out a bit by saying, with a quite unaccustomed edge to her voice, "He's gone off and left us to join the gypsies."

My grandfather — something clicked when he heard the word — fixed us all what with what had become his familiar beatific smile and intoned:

> What care I for a goose-feather bed
> With the sheet turned down so bravely, O?
> For tonight I shall sleep in a cold open field
> Along with the raggle-taggle gypsies, O!

"Okaaaay," said my cousin Jane. Nice kid, smart kid, and I liked her, but after four years of college, an M.A., and all the prospects in the world open to her, the only way she knew how to respond to anything outside the range of the acceptable, outside the Pale as it were, was with that outwardly skeptical, inwardly frightened "okaaaay."

I didn't know what to say to them, so I talked about long lost friends of mine from the old neighborhood, old friends, not really gypsies — I should have gone with the commune story — stalling, stalling, talking about the woods, the horses, putting off questions, putting them aside. In the end, it didn't matter, their comprehension or incomprehension didn't matter much to them or to me. We were always good for sharing a laugh together anyway.

They let me go after a good-natured inquisition and moved on to other things, but my cousin Jane, did ask, after I described the dark beauty of the old woods, "Whatever did you come home for?"

"For my mother's hard sauce and Uncle Joe's eggnog," I said.

"So for an early heart attack, you're saying."

All the time I was with the Dragons and the Cats, I don't remember a one of them talking about his cholesterol level.

While I was home, I got my pipes going again. As usual, I felt as if I was rebuilding, recovering lost ground instead of progressing. I worked on the same faults, and corrected the same mistakes, as I'd done a year ago. I'd had excellent instruction from a man who lived over the mountains, unconnected to our college, but I was not a good piper. I suppose I was adequate for the length of time I'd played and practiced; adequate, but no better. It was the same with my fencing; I was adequate (at least until Thomas the Rhymer got hold of me.) Even as a classicist, in my own view, I was adequate, no better. I'd graduated with honors from a top school, but push-come-to-shove, I think my grandfather, even in his failing stages, still had a better feeling for Latin and Greek, and certainly a better memory for what he'd studied, than I did.

I seemed to be condemned to mediocrity in all my endeavors. I brought up this concern to Cornelia once, and she immediately responded by dubbing me "Sir James Prettygood." But when she saw I took the idea at least semi-seriously, she said:

"For someone to really get good at something, he has to lose everything else. You have to be simple-minded, I mean *single*-minded. Maybe you haven't found want you want to be really good at yet. Or maybe you'll find a role where it's good to be a generalist, a jack-of-all-trades."

She did take to calling me, Sir James, though, our little joke.

I spent a lot of time working over Thomas' *"Fechtbuch,"* his fencing manual, often up in my bedroom, just as I used to swing the nunchucks I'd picked up in Flushing years before, trying to learn by myself with the aid of a book. Some of the illustrations were familiar, but many of them described maneuvers and concepts I hadn't yet learned. I used a stick, an old epee, and when I was in close quarters, even a ruler. It was the footwork that determined the sword placement and subsequent use of the blade, but it was just there, in determining the stances and steps, that I found the pictures least useful. The drawings were there for a reminder, I realized, not for cold instruction. I tried to use them to revive what I'd learned from the master directly. I practiced outside when I could, but the snow and the mud and the cold too often made that impossible.

I also learned to drive. I got my learner's permit and took lessons from a guy named Jose ("now we gonna lerng to do a broking-a u-turn"). He was an efficient and experienced teacher, and I learned well despite the often snow-narrowed streets on which we drove, but I didn't have time enough to schedule and take my test before I left again for Pennsylvania. I would have passed.

The invitation arrived in mid-March. I'd gotten a few gossipy letters from Cornelia over the break, and a home-made hand-painted Christmas card signed by her and her mother. They moved around down south, in North Carolina for a while, but eventually all the way down to Florida. They did not move randomly, I'd learned, but passed through familiar locations, where they were likely to find friends and relatives, some settled, some not. There hadn't been any mention of the future and my return until this letter in March.

It was still cold in Pennsylvania, Cornelia explained, but Aunt Vivien was planning to go up this year in early April. The Cats were going too, Cornelia said, and if I liked, I could come out and help them get the place — that is Dragon Town — ready for Aunt Vivien's arrival. I didn't quite know what to make of this, but it would get me out to Dragon Town in the spring, so I sent back that I'd be happy to go, if someone could tell me how to get there.

My parents were not surprised, when I told them. My father might even have been pleased. I think he believed that the Dragons had a good, one could say a *bracing* influence on me. After all, they were his people too. My mother took the news with a minimum of fuss and comment, but as one who was pointedly keeping her own counsel.

My sister, when I told her, was seated at the piano, and immediately started playing, "The Bells are Ringing, For Me and My Gal."

A few days later, when we were alone in the kitchen, my mother asked me, "So you like this Cornelia?"

"Yes."

"Are you going to marry her?"

I was shocked by this direct and unexpected question. I hemmed, I hawed. Well I don't know … I wasn't thinking … We just … trailing off at last down the escape route of indulgent laughter.

"It's not such an outlandish question," my mother said and went back to her work.

I would have liked to see her together with Mrs. Parsons, I thought, watching her back as she chopped celery and carrots. I was sure they'd get along.

9. Two Visits

1.

The drive to Dragon Town was easily arranged. The Dragons had begun their move back to New York in earnest, and there was no lack of traffic into and out of the city. They had even opened up the Big House, just around the corner. Mattheus was staying there, and when it was time for me to go, it was Mattheus who drove me. We were not alone; Mr. Dillon sat in the back, accompanied by his papers and files which he spread, slid and arranged across the back seat. He was the new style lawyer, the man I would be working with if I accepted the Dragons' offer to send me to law school.

Mr. Dillon was a middle-aged, sun-darkened, heavy-set man with keen grey eyes and short dark hair. He did not fit any of my stereotypes of a lawyer; if someone had told me he had recently retired from the Foreign Legion I might have believed it. Mr. Dillon kept up a sporadic commentary from the back seat. It was difficult to follow the thread of his remarks, since his casual mumble was easily swallowed in the ambient noise of traffic and a good deal of the time his comments were inspired by the papers he had before him, unseen by and in any case unintelligible to Mattheus and myself. Sometimes I would respond to a remark that turned out to be part of a private monologue and Mr. Dillon, surprised by my voice and not properly hearing my words, would look up and say, "Eh?" We had a lot of pointless cross-talk before I caught on to his back-seat conversational style. Mattheus, used to driving him around, simply dispensed himself from paying attention to anything not unambiguously addressed to him. If Mr. Dillon wanted to say something to you, you'd know it.

Toward the end of our journey, as we passed out of New Jersey and into Pennsylvania, Mr. Dillon did engage me in direct extended conversation. He was very pleasant, but he asked a lot of questions, about school, about my favorite courses, about my interests and reading habits, and I got the impression that I was, however gently, being interviewed.

We rolled into Dragon Town in the late afternoon, avoiding rush hour at both ends of the trip. We parked in front of the guard house. Sure enough, the grey dog, Fergus, came out on the front porch to greet us, closely followed by the woman of the house. She had spent the winter there, running a lonely port of call for any of the three tribes who happened to wander through the area. She was not a demonstrative woman, a tall, strong, sandy-haired woman in a thick ropy sweater, but I think she was glad to see us. We were among the first arrivals back in town; it was early April. The driveway and footpaths were covered by last fall's leaves mashed into mud, and the snow lingered in the shade of the deep woods.

I brought my gear to the bunkhouse. It had been closed much of the winter and the smell of clean cut wood was strong. We ate supper together up at the guard house, seated around the kitchen table. It was a comfortable meal, just the three of us travelers and our hostess. Mrs. Hughes, that was the woman of the house, always had food at the ready for visitors. She sat at the head of the table, her thick hair glowing in the light of the two bare kitchen bulbs, attended by Fergus, who appeared to be taking an intelligent interest in the conversation. He did about as well as I, since they spoke mostly in their own tongue, forgetting about my limitations, except when Mr. Dillon steered the conversation into English. I learned that Miss Widdershins and Thomas were staying over at the Cats' campground waiting for Dragon Town to be put ready for their arrival and enjoying something of a spring idyll.

I turned in early. The dog walked me back, looking up from time to time as if he were about to address me or expected me to say something to him. He left me at the door. The bunkhouse was cold, but there were blankets and a broad quilt for my bed. I was disappointed that I hadn't seen nor heard anything of Cornelia, but I was glad to be back in my old room, listening to the night sounds, the creaking of the wood planks and the rustling of the spring trees, and the wind playing across it all.

I awoke late. Wintering in Queens, I'd lost the habit of rising early. When I emerged from the bunkhouse, I was delighted to see Cornelia's trailer parked across the path. Someone had backed it in, unhitched it and driven away, all without waking me up. I crossed the path, climbed the wooden steps, and knocked, while all about me Cornelia's painted big-nosed wood-elves gamboled through the trees on the side of the caravan and above the lintel. There was no answer; the Parsons were already out and about.

I walked up to the guardhouse, hoping for some breakfast and some news. When I opened the door I saw Mrs. Parsons sitting at the kitchen table, smoking a slender cigarillo and holding forth on some subject while Mrs. Hughes wiped and dried the breakfast dishes.

"James!" she said. "They told us you were here. Cornelia's up at the Castle. We're sprucing up the place. Go join her, she'll find something for you to do."

"Wait, wait." Mrs. Hughes dried her hands. "Have something to eat first."

She brought a croissant out of a white bakery bag. Someone had already been to town. I ate it leaning over the trash bin to catch the falling flakes, and was about to go when she pressed a cup of coffee on me. So I sat at the table and ate another pastry.

"Have you been to the camp yet to see Clan Arthur?"

"No, we came straight here yesterday."

"We'll take you over later this afternoon. It's still quiet here, and there. A late spring … everyone is straggling in."

I finished fast as I could and hurried up toward the castle. The town square was empty, and I thought at first the place was deserted, but I heard a window being opened in one of the little huts to the right and I saw a thin slow spiral of smoke rising from the refectory chimney. The place was awakening from its long winter's nap, a buried city coming to life, a Germelshausen.

I kicked up the turning path through last season's leaves and then through the final gate, and I was back in the old courtyard. Someone had already been there, hard at work; it was swept and cleaned, bundles of tied sticks against the curtain wall, and bags of leaves stacked. I looked all about for a sign of Cornelia, and caught a movement in the Keep's second floor window. There she was, and she had seen me now and leaned out waving a broom. With a long spotted gabled kerchief binding her hair, and a sturdy thick-handled broom in her hand, she looked like she was about to fly off the page of a German children's book.

I called up to her:

> *"Old woman, old woman, old woman, said I*
> *Whither, O whither, O whither so high?"*

She called back:

> *"To sweep the cobwebs from out of the sky*
> *And I'll be with you, by and by."*

I went up and joined her in the Keep.

2.

The next few days were great fun. It reminded me of nothing so much as the last day of the grammar school year, when we would come to school in our street clothes and sneakers, and clean out our desks and throw rags soaked in sweet-smelling cleanser around the room, as if the wild freedom of summer had been let in the open windows and at any moment vines would start growing in and around the desks and boards. Cornelia and I spent the first couple of days up at the Castle. The open floors of the Keep needed a lot of cleaning, and we had to bring books and furnishings up the winding stairs, which wasn't easy. We didn't know where everything was supposed to go, but Garn showed up the second day to help direct us. He was butler as well as the general foreman. When we finished with the Keep we opened up the cozy cottage.

We readied the kitchen, plumped up the beds, and brought new toys into Arthur's room, laying a stuffed green dragon on his pillow. We even got to hang the Vermeer, on the white wall between the bedrooms, as it had been at the Big House.

Every day the place got livelier, as the new arrivals took up their work. We started to turn over the soil for the garden, and I was brought outdoors while Cornelia stayed inside, moving from one house to another, helping as each set up his home or workshop. I spent some time up around the sun bower, clearing out the sunken hearths, tapping shingles down on the roof, slathering on a new coat of wood preserver. Everywhere was the sound of digging, scraping, polishing, moving, firing and most of all singing. We all sang at our work, and I learned a lot of new songs that week. I don't remember getting tired.

As it turned out, Mrs. Parsons did not take us to visit Clan Arthur that first afternoon. It was a full week later when we rolled up the lane. We stopped halfway down, and stepped out into the pale greengold light of the spring trees.

"So, let's see what they've done with the old place," Cornelia said.

It was like entering a lonely forest glade. It was easy to forget that there were houses and streets and all the ordinary trappings of ordinary life only a short distance away through the trees. Only one trailer stood in the clearing, the large vehicle that had served as the royal residence last year, parked in the same place next to the boulder. A single big pavilion was pitched off to the right, facing the trailer across the main fire pit, covered in a deep blue silk decorated with yellow flowers and with a canopy over the door and a red pennon twirling from a pole at the spire. It was there they received visitors and conducted their business.

Thomas was out on the ground, swinging a staff, now slow, now fast, now in great swooping movements, now in quick sharp thrusts. I had never seen him use a staff before. It looked like he was performing a kata. I wondered, was this something he had picked up from an Asian martial art, was it something he'd made up himself, or was it something from the dim past of Europe, long forgotten by the Bellymen, treasured only by these tribes, hearkening back to the Salmon Leaps and Apple Feats of the Hound of Ulster? He did not look up to see us.

Miss Widdershins appeared in the trailer doorway.

"You're here! Let me just put my shoes on."

I remembered from the old days that she favored bare feet when the terrain allowed. She soon came out in little low silver slippers.

"So good to see you all here again." She linked arms with Mrs. Parsons. In her slippers she stood even with Cornelia's petite mother. I looked down at her as we walked together across the spring clearing. With her long blonde hair, framed with a single thin braid that circled her head and trailed behind, with her elemental female physique draped in a simple rough sack dress, she looked the part of a hippy chick, ripened with age, welcoming us to her upstate artist's colony.

Cornelia meanwhile was looking all around us.

"Where's Arthur?" she demanded.

"He's still down state. He was worried about Fernando, his pony. He'd hurt his leg on a fence and Arthur wanted to travel with him. He's staying with Cassie, and Balin's with him, and Dolores of course."

"Of course." Thomas had come up and joined us, leaning on his staff.

"So for a few days, we are on our own. I get to enjoy a little stay in Arcadia alone with my Naoise," and Miss Widdershins reached up and caressed her husband's rough cheek.

It was obvious she was enjoying herself immensely. The clearing was coming to life with the season. The damp earth was speckled with white violets and yellow cowslips and assorted other wildflowers in sprays and bells and disks. It was still too early for bugs to be a nuisance.

We stepped under the entrance canopy into the blue light of the pavilion. We sat on benches and ate strawberries brought up from the south, and cakes and fresh whipped cream. Miss Widdershins drank wine, for all it was so early in the day, and Thomas kept her company. The rest of us sipped tea or water.

They gossiped for a while, mostly about people I didn't know. Siobhán had given birth, a little boy. Colin was out in Michigan.

Something tripped my memory, and I said to Thomas, "Oh, I have your *fechtbuch* in the car. I wanted to give it back to you."

"Keep it," he said. "I've changed my philosophy since those days. No more books and techniques for me. Was it any use to you?"

"Yes. Especially with the stuff you showed me; it helped me

remember. I wasn't sure about figuring out any new moves."

"Yes, that's a problem. It's more of a memory aid."

"I couldn't tell if I was on the right track or not."

"We'll go over it together."

They said they'd be moving over to the Castle in a few days, probably before Easter.

"It's ready for you," said Cornelia. "The joint is jumpin'."

When we were finished with our meal and our talk, they walked us back to the car.

"I miss Arthur," Cornelia said. "I was looking forward to seeing my crazy little bear cub."

"Oh, I miss him too. He'll be up any day now."

We stood for a while around the car making our final goodbyes. I noticed Thomas was smiling, as if he was laughing at me.

"What?" I asked. "What's so funny?"

Thomas smiled broader.

"You still call my wife 'Miss Widdershins'."

"Oh. I guess I do. I hadn't thought about it. What should I call you?" I asked her directly.

"Miss Widdershins is fine." She squeezed my arm. "It's a nice reminder of the old days in New York. They were good days, for all the troubles we had."

At last we got in the car and drove away.

3.

Three days later, early Friday morning, I awoke to the sound of Cornelia wailing. It was still dark in my room. I did not know at first what sound I was hearing, or even that I was hearing a sound. I was only conscious of an immense unquiet, as if I were in the midst of a terrible dream, but I was awake. I rose and pulled on my pants and my shoes, all the while trying to put order and meaning to my sensations.

By the time I was halfway down the hall, I knew I was hearing a person crying, and by the time I reached the front door, I knew it was Cornelia. I pushed the door open and stepped out into the cold dawn air to see her collapsed at the foot of her trailer's steps, and her mother by her side with her arms wrapped around her.

I ran over to her, calling out "What happened? What happened?"

"They're dead!" Cornelia wailed. She looked up and her face and hair were wet with tears.

"Who? What?"

"They're dead! My love, my queen, my auntie!"

Her mother gripped her hard. I heard, or rather felt, a roaring in my ears, and knelt on the ground next to them as if I could not stand.

"How? How? Why?"

Cornelia rocked and moaned and her mother answered.

"The police came in the early morning, before dawn. They raided the caravan and the campground. My brother and Vivien were asleep."

"The police? But why?"

"Police, federals... there were many, many. They were seen. Some of our people were camped nearby."

"But why? And why did they kill them""

"My brother fought. It is his nature. And the Queen. Ohhh!" and she began to moan with Cornelia and they rocked together, lamenting in their own tongue. I put my arms around them and rocked with them.

Of a sudden, I felt that there was someone standing over us, and I leaped to my feet. It was Mr. Dillon. He looked as stunned as the others, but he had work on his mind.

"You have heard," he said.

I thought I could get something from him, facts, something to make it all into sense. I even thought that if there had been some mistake, he would be the man to sort it out.

"What happened? Is it true?"

"It's true."

"Why? Why did it happen?"

"That's a question for later. I think it was a misdirected raid, prompted by malice, theirs or someone else's. It was an invasion. There were federal agents present along with the sheriff's department. We'll figure it out later. Now, we have to act. They will be coming *here* soon. It will not take them long to discover that Vivien and Thomas were based here, that their real residence is here. They will be coming here and they will be coming hard. There were lawmen killed too, at least two, possibly more. Now there are things here that we can't let them see and things here that we don't wish for them to have. The book, the painting, other things. If we don't get them out now before the law comes, then we will have to fight here, and we are undermanned. I need your help.

Come with me now, I'll tell you what to take and where to take it. I wish Dinan were here, he could see to the townsfolk."

"Go," said Mrs. Parsons.

"I'm ready," I said. Then a terrible thought came to me. "What about Arthur?"

"The King is safe," said Dillon. "He had not yet joined them. He's with his people, God help him. Now, I need strong young people. Cornelia?"

"I can't!" Cornelia wailed, and I do believe that it would not have been possible at that moment for her to walk or stand.

"That's all right, love," said Dillon kindly. "Just mourn and pray." Then, to me, "Come."

We went.

The floodlights outside the guardhouse and over the town gate threw an unnatural glare over everything, like a form of hysteria. The news had spread, and the townspeople were milling about the square; the doors to their little huts and houses stood open. We walked through the square and it was like a perfect nightmare. People were crying and kneeling and clutching one another, and one poor old woman, who helped out at the refectory, had thrown her apron over her head and was screaming. Mrs. Hughes was with her, trying to calm her, and the dog was looking at her, whining and yelping and setting up to howl. I was no different from the others; I felt what they felt.

I followed Dillon up the path toward the Castle, the familiar path between the walls. Even that first night I thought how terribly sad it was, how everything had changed just that morning, how this path that had once led to a refuge of peace and happiness was now bringing me to an unknown world that promised only sorrow and fear. They could not have suffered a disaster like this for a long long time, the Dragons, not since before they'd come to America, maybe not since they'd left Ireland. Maybe before that.

We went to the Keep first. Dillon lit the lamps and climbed up to the second floor, while I remained below. The great book, the Black Book of Leuven was waiting closed and latched on the table. We'd set it up to be ready for Miss Widdershins' arrival, since she was so fond of it and often had occasion to consult it, but now it would have to be moved again, and fast.

Dillon came down with a leather file of folders slung over his shoulder.

"First, wrap the book," he said.

I knew how to do that and knew where the wrapping was, in a cupboard against the wall, because I had helped unwrap it a few days ago.

Dillon helped me, for it was a great heavy book, and we had to lift and turn it while we swaddled it in a soft dark cloth, what I took to be some kind of oilcloth. When we finished, we buckled the oilcloth securely. There were straps attached that allowed the book to be carried over a person's back.

All the while Dillon was talking.

"I've sent Mattheus around in a car. There's a path that leads out behind the garden, along the side of the ridge and then over and down to a hidden drive. Mattheus will be waiting there. You've never been there, I think, and you won't be able to follow it alone in the dark. I'll have to go with you. That's going to slow us up. There's no help for it. We'll have to make many trips. Oh, good, Cornelia, you're here."

Cornelia had entered the keep and stood beside me. Her cheeks were still wet, but she had recovered herself and was ready to help.

They loaded the book on my back, and I hooked my arms through the straps. Then Dillon gave Cornelia the leather file box, and some more papers and sent us on our way.

"Hurry back."

Cornelia led me out the postern gate, and around the outskirts of the newly turned garden, then up a narrow road that ran along the side of the ridge dividing us from the main road. I recognized the path. It was a peaceful spot; I would sometimes lie up here, where the ferns grew thickest, and gaze out with gratitude and pride over the castle and the fairy tale town beyond. I'd never followed it to the end. The trees grew taller and closer, then the ridge bent to the right, and we climbed over it. As I passed the summit I looked down and saw Mattheus standing beside his car, at the foot of a steep drop. When we got down to the car, we unhooked the book and laid it in the open trunk. We left it to Mattheus to stow Cornelia's leather file case and papers and ran back to the Keep.

Dillon had the books and papers already arranged on the table for us. We were limited in what we could carry by the lack of bags or containers. We had to make two more trips to clear the table, hurrying over the path, back and forth, with our heads down, breathing hard. As we departed on the second of these trips, Dillon said, "That's all for the Keep. When you come back, come to the cottage."

It was very sad walking into that spruce, scrubbed, cozy little cottage with the purpose that we had. The first order of business was the painting on the wall. They had a case for that, another leather and oilskin carrying system, which had helped keep it safe for four centuries. There were personal effects, bits of jewelry, insignia of rank, which we gathered up as well. Here we could use pillow cases to transport those loose items that were not breakable.

As we left from the cottage the first time, Dillon said, "You know this house better than I. Take whatever we need to keep hidden. And try to remove anything that shows a child was coming here. The first order of business is to protect the King. If they know there was a child orphaned they will try to take him. I've got to get back to the town. I'm sure Garn and Lizzie Hughes have their hands full. We want to get our people cleared from out of here, as many as we can. We can't have them being questioned. Most of them have no papers, no records of any kind. I've got my work cut out for me... They've got no right to come in here and grab people, but they'll do it anyway. And with policemen killed... No, we had better not stand on our rights. You two can drive out with Mattheus; there should be room in the car."

"No, I'm going back to Mama. I told her I'd come back."

I remembered — a quick vision — coming out of the bunkhouse and seeing Mrs. Parsons with her arms around Cornelia at the foot of the steps. She had just lost her brother, but even in that extremity her first concern was to comfort her daughter.

Cornelia was crying again when we started down the path laden with cottage treasures, so lately brought and arranged by us to make a graceful and happy life for the royal family. When we went back the second time, we ran throughout the house, looking for anything intended for Arthur. A few picture books, some toys and games, a set of blocks, and we were gone. We wrapped them up in a sheet swept off the master bed, and at the last, Cornelia took the great big stuffed dragon we'd put on Arthur's little bed. I remember, Cornelia had wanted to be there when he first saw it. I walked down the trail that last time hearing Cornelia's muffled sobs and watching the dragon's plush head bobbing over her shoulder.

We had cleared the two buildings, but overlooked Arthur's plastic car, which was sitting out of sight among the trees and benches in the center of the courtyard. That would be enough to tell our enemies that a child had been there, but not, perhaps, enough to indicate that a child ever lived there on a permanent basis, or that the child was the offspring of their two victims and thus might be considered their rightful spoil. We probably slipped up on a few other things, but all in all I think we did well.

We crammed Arthur's possessions into the back seat and put the dragon over it all. When we were finished, I stood with Cornelia at the back of the car.

"I'll pick up your gear from the bunkhouse," she said. "We'll take it with us."

Then she shook her head.

"We've lost our heart and our strength," she said. "From one day to another. We've lost more… " but she fell silent.

We put our arms around each other and clung to each other for what seemed like a long time. She put her head on my shoulder and pressed her wet hair and wetter cheek to my face. At last she pushed me away.

"I have to go," she said, and turned back to the trail.

I got in the car alongside Mattheus. He alone of the Dragons, aside from the lawyer Dillon who was trained for disaster, seemed not to have been knocked off his center by this catastrophe. Perhaps his innate melancholy — which I had noticed when I first met him, even under the happy circumstance of a release from prison — perhaps this melancholy disposed him to expect sudden reversals of fate and not to be overthrown by them. Or perhaps it only helped him conceal the depths of his feelings, from others, from himself.

"Is that everything?" he asked.

"Yes. Everything we can do."

It was full morning now. The car began to roll slowly down the rutted path through the woods. An old creaky car, of a boxy build not seen in new models for twenty years, with one off-color fender, and loaded with jewelry, antique weaponry, rare books and one painting worth by itself at least one hundred million dollars. And one stuffed dragon. All of it chosen by us not for its monetary value, but for its association with our people, with the old tribe.

We reached the end of the wooded path, paused, looked for traffic that was not there, and turned onto the paved road.

10. The Great Gathering

1.

We drove for a long time. Mattheus brought us onto the turnpike and for a while we slipped in among the big rigs hurrying about their business. Then he turned south. He knew where we were going but I didn't. Neither of us spoke. I thought about all I was leaving behind, further and further away. I wondered what Cornelia was doing, and her mother, and how the rest of us were faring back in the town. Had the police yet forced their entry?

We left the state. The ground got higher and the driving got slower. Then, at a place that looked no different from a hundred places we had passed, Mattheus turned off the road onto a grassy path. It led us past raised borders of trees, almost like Normandy hedgerows, and deposited us in a wide field, out of sight of the road. Mattheus drove across the field and parked at the edge, up against a dense wood.

"We're here," said Mattheus. He got out of the car and I did the same.

"What now?" I asked.

"The others should be arriving soon. This is one of our gathering places. After they get here, I've got to take this stuff further south."

"Who is coming?"

"People from the south and west. People from Pennsylvania, from the Northeast Summer ground. Cornelia and her mother will be here. We've got a motel we use, just a few hundred yards away. The King will be staying there I expect, with Cassie and Dolores. And Balin."

"What about Dillon?"

"He's got to stay on site. He'll send messengers. He's in charge for the time being."

We waited in silence. There was nothing to do but lean on the car and smoke or lie in the grass and stare at the sky.

It wasn't long, not more than an hour, I guessed, before a second car rolled into the field, closely followed by two others. They came to a stop at the edge of the grass next to us, and when the doors opened and the passengers issued forth, I saw that I recognized not a one of them. It was the first intimation of the flood of Dragons that was about to pour into this corner of the country, more than I imagined there could be. The women, at the sight of new countrymen with whom to share their sorrow, broke into fresh bouts of weeping and embraced us both, the glum men shook hands in silence.

When Mattheus told them who I was, one of the women, a small plush party with a long braid said, "Oh, you're Cornelia's young man. Dear Cornelia," and embraced me as fervently as if she were hugging the dear one of whom she spoke.

They brought food, mostly bread, cheese, and ale, and we sat on the grass and ate off spread cloths. One of the cars had been towing a trailer, and after we finished eating they opened this up and began unpacking the elements of a tent. I helped by pulling on the guy ropes where instructed, and in no time they had the structure up and secured. If they slept close, I thought, they could sleep a dozen inside.

While we were finishing this task, some other cars drove into the field, and parked in line with us. I thought at first that I didn't recognize any of these either, but one of them, a youngish man, when he shook my hand, jogged my memory.

"You probably don't remember me," he said. "I was in the house the day we settled with Gone-Away. I was at the other end of the couch." I remembered him then. I had thought that he looked like a tired college kid, but he looked now like a soldier, like he might be one of Troll's friends. He told me his name was Dónall. A lot of us were named Dónall or Donald, it turned out. He was Dónall Pats or Dónall Óg.

They kept arriving. More tents, of varying sizes, were erected. Someone got a camp stove going, an aluminum and gas affair, and started doling out stew. At last my people arrived, people from Dragon Town and the Cats' camp, with Cornelia's trailer bringing up the rear. Mattie Donald drove the truck and Mrs. Parson sat alongside him, smoking one of her little cigars. It was not the full population by any means; most had stayed behind with Mr. Dillon, Mrs. Hughes and Garn.

These latest arrivals drew a crowd. They were the ones with first hand news, who might be able to tell what had happened and how and why. The other Dragons had pumped me for information, but I had little to give them beyond what they already knew. But they thought perhaps these new arrivals had learned more in the hours since Mattheus and I had left Dragon Town. I joined the others as we stood in a semicircle around the newly arrived vehicles.

As usual, Mrs. Parsons took the lead role. You could tell she would do so just from the way she climbed down out of the truck, conscious that all eyes were on her. For her part, Cornelia jumped down from the trailer without bothering to set the wooden steps. She ran over and stood beside me. While Mrs. Parsons addressed the crowd, Cornelia spoke to me only.

"How long have you been here?" Cornelia asked.

"Just a few hours. I don't have a watch. About three hours, I think."

"We got out fast. Before any police arrived. But we had to wait for the others to get themselves together. We wanted to travel in a *buion*, in a group. We pulled over by the side of the road until they came."

"Do you know all these people?" I asked indicating the crowd of listeners.

"I think so. I've seen them all anyway at one time or another."

"So did the police ever show at the town, do you know?"

"I don't know. Once the others caught up to us, we hit the road and kept driving. We haven't talked to them since."

"So what happened? What really happened?"

Cornelia had her arm linked through mine, and we brought our heads close together as she talked. All this time, little Mrs. Parsons was addressing the Dragons with the same information Cornelia was giving me.

"A lot of it is still a mystery. There are a lot of questions still.

That's something I have to talk to you about. Dillon has an assignment for you. What we know, there was a raid just before dawn. It was planned and prepared. There were police, and people from the sheriff's office, and *federales* too, both DEA and ATF agents. It was crazy. Mattie thinks there were thirty people there, and more after it was all over. They just broke into Aunt Vivien's trailer with helmets and armor and shields and guns, shouting and screaming. They must have woken Aunt Vivien and Uncle Tom up — they sleep late when they sleep together — and Uncle Tom must have fought. He died first; then Aunt Vivien. They heard her scream his name before she died. They got two of the cops anyway, at least. After that the cars came from all over, and helicopters too."

"But why? I still don't know why."

"Dillon figures, from the composition of the attacking force," I could tell she was quoting him directly, "that they must have gotten a tip that Aunt Vivien and Uncle Tom were dealing drugs or arms out of the trailer. Or both. But right now that's just a guess. But I think it's a good one."

"Are you serious? Why would anyone believe that?"

"People always believe the worst about us."

I thought about it. The constant stream of people coming and going, often with packages, and traveling in and out of state, driving long distances. It would give color to an accusation. But first someone would have to bring the accusation.

"But someone would have to start this. Someone would have had to sic the police on them."

Cornelia nodded. We looked at each other and already suspicion had begun to form. The dirtbags in the white houses.

"We don't know who. But we'll find out. Dillon wants your help. He wants you to wait in the motel — we have a place near here — and watch everything you can on the news that mentions us. Not just what the police say, the official reports, but see who gets interviewed, who shows up on camera, who is standing around in the background. Get the local newspapers too. He thinks you'd be the best to know how to interpret them, 'cause you used to live with the Bellymen. In the meantime, he'll try to get at the police reports. The Geese should help out with that. I have my own thoughts..."

"Yeah."

"But we need to know."

2.

Mrs. Parsons had finished her explanation at about the same time as Cornelia. We all milled around, gathering into small murmuring groups that shifted and reformed. The mood had subtly shifted away from pure sorrow, and I felt a heavy anger, a subtle undercurrent with an ominous potential to strengthen. I had never seen so many of us gathered, and it so quiet, with no laughter and no song.

I found myself back with Mattheus. I told him what Cornelia had told me, that I was to go to the motel. He gave me directions; as he'd said, it wasn't far.

"I can drive you if you don't mind waiting," he said.

But I wanted out. The tense atmosphere, without any possibility of action, was swiftly becoming unbearable to me. I found Cornelia, standing silently with a group of shorter, older women, and told her I was going to the motel.

"I'll get you your gear," she said.

I followed her inside the trailer. It was chaotic, piled everywhere with other people's belongings. She pulled my heavy pack off the couch and made as if to load it on my back.

"Wait a second. Where's my other bag, my … it's like a satchel."

That was also on the couch. I opened it and looked through it, shuffling through books and papers. I moved aside the Rhymer's manual of arms, and thought for a moment of the gentle, violent man who had given it to me. I found what I was looking for, an empty spiral pad with a blue Bic shoved into the spirals. I had brought it intending to record my impressions on this my second sojourn with the Dragons, to copy down songs, to record new words and memorialize great moments. Now I thought it would be useful to keep and order whatever information I discovered from the news. Whatever would help us with the coming hunt. I crammed it into the back pocket of my pack and then dipped, while Cornelia helped load the heavy burden onto my back. I had a time getting out the door and down to the ground without the wooden steps.

"Well, I'm off."

"We're staying around here with the trailer. I'll probably come by and see you soon."

She gave me a quick hug and a kiss in a somewhat abstracted way, as if I were a husband going off to work in the morning and she had a lot of errands to run during the day. Even in the midst of that day's desolation, I found that rather endearing.

I started off walking. Just when I got to the end of the field, where the border of trees began, I had to step aside for a small convoy, three old, long-bodied cars followed by a pickup towing a horse trailer. I turned and watched them. Everyone in the field stopped what they were doing and turned to watch them. It was Arthur, the king, and his retinue. They parked in the middle of the field and the crowd gathered. Balin got out of the second car, easily recognized even from a distance. From the first car, I thought I recognized Cassie, the red-haired woman who was Miss Widdershins' cousin, and whom I had seen seven, now eight years ago. She got out and turned back to the car, and then I saw Arthur climb down to the grass. I didn't know whether they'd told him. I didn't want to know. I had no idea how a person told a child something like that — that his parents, his sun, moon and sky, the very earth beneath his feet, had vanished from his life forever.

Arthur looked around at the wall of people, and found what he was looking for, his still safe haven. He ran over to Cornelia as I had seen him do in the courtyard, a few months and an age ago, and she gathered him in. I thought then from the way he ran that they had told him.

I turned away from them again and walked toward the motel. When I got out of the lane and back on the hardtop, I turned left, as Matthaeus had told me. I kept to the shoulder, unremarked and mostly unnoticed by the passing autos, the latest in a long line of Dragons left to brood on treachery and loss in the dust of the road.

3.

𝐼 spent most of the next few days lying on the bumpy coverlet of a motel bed, watching television and taking notes. Every day, I'd walk down the road to a nearby convenience store and sweep up whatever passed for a newspaper, free and for pay, local and national. It was intelligence gathering of the most basic kind, but it was necessary. Without it there was no one in the tribe who was plugged-in, and we needed to know what the Bellymen were saying.

On television, I kept seeing the same scenes, the same spokesmen, the same snippets of the same news conferences. I saw the same interviews with the same ersatz witnesses. None of the neighbors had seen the events as they happened, since the whole fight took place on the Cats' campground, but some of them had plenty to say nevertheless.

The official story as it emerged was more or less what we expected. There was a multi-agency operational group "tasked," so they said, with stamping out a drug epidemic in the area, which had seen many young people taken to the emergency room and many young lives lost or ruined. So they said. In the course of this operation a confidential informant told them about the drugs and arms — I guess he threw in the arms as a bonus — being sold out of Miss Widdershins' trailer. I didn't know the motive for the absurd lie, but I could guess a few possibilities. An actual drug dealer looking to deflect attention from himself, a dirtbag looking for revenge for his dog, or simply a fool voicing his suspicions as certainties. We wouldn't know for sure until we found out who the informant was. Law enforcement wasn't saying, and reporters weren't asking.

"After placing the premises under surveillance and observing suspicious activity," the multi-agency task force staged a raid in the early morning. And got more than they bargained for. If things had gone the way they expected, they would have ripped through the door, all dolled up in their flak jackets and black gloves and helmets, shining lights, carrying guns and shields, shouting "get on the ground," "put your hands behind your head," and other old favorites, while the householders cowered on the floor and wet themselves. If they were guilty, all to the good; if they were innocent, no harm done. Frankly, when I saw the representatives of the various agencies taking their turns at the microphone, deferring to one another, each praising the other's professionalism and dedication, it came to me that the whole thing may have been originally viewed in the light of a joint military exercise, a training run, like one of those NATO exercises by land, sea and air. Professionalism proved, technique refined, camaraderie built and never an angry shot fired or received.

Instead, they got Thomas the Rhymer. The authorities never came through with a blow-by-blow, and the reporters never pressed, but we got the inside scoop from the Geese, who could still work the old network when they needed information, through how many degrees of separation I didn't know. Mattie Donald came to the motel and told a bunch of us, gathered in one room, hungry for the story.

"They were still in bed when it happened. The cops popped the lock and came running in shouting. Thomas just grabbed that old single edge — he must have been polishing it or something it was next to the bed — and launched himself at the first guy through the door. They opened up on him, but you know how fast he was. He put that blade through the guy's plastic visor, through his skull, and out the back of his helmet. They must have had a hell of a time pulling it out of his head later."

"The Lady saw all this. She might have been hit by the first shots. She screamed his name, reached for — you know that varmint gun they had — and got one shot off before they killed her. One shot and she hit the second guy right in the neck. Then they blew them both to pieces."

We rolled this around in our minds. In the midst of our horror, we were pleased that they had both gotten their man. I had no thought to spare for the dead law officers as their comrades had no thought for the two they had killed. It was the old enemy again, in a new guise, doing what he did.

I can't say I learned a great deal of useful information during those days in the motel, but I did learn a lot about the way the news works. From the first reports of the tragic incident — "on a quiet morning in rural Pennsylvania we got a stark reminder that the men and women in uniform who protect our lives and freedoms put their own lives on the line for us every day" — I heard no one question the official version of events. "We were reminded that the War on Drugs is a real war with real casualties," where the irony, I think, was purely unintentional. They went along with the "weapons" aspect too. I can't count how many times I saw the same "cache" of weapons discovered at the trailer, a cache displayed in an artfully deceptive manner, with the view showing the entirety of their meagre collection while suggesting that there was more that didn't fit into the frame. I recognized a single shot, literally single shot, .25 caliber rifle used for small game, a single-edge sword from eighteenth century Scotland that had been polished and sharpened so many times over the years that it had shrunk to resemble an oversized awl, and a big hunting knife, one of a set of implements acquired, I believe, in Bavaria some time in the long ago.

Once the neighbors got involved, that is, once they started giving interviews, we started hearing about Miss Widdershins and Thomas as "separatists," which, I suppose was true, but it wasn't long before the simple separatists became "white separatists," which again, I suppose, was largely true but more as a matter of historical fact than of policy. The shadowy border between white separatism and white supremacy was easy to erase in the mind of viewer and performer alike, and the impression of meth-cooking gun-toting savages, twisted by hatred and determined to die in a last-ditch shootout, is the one that remained and solidified into hard fact.

I took a certain amount of bitter satisfaction in observing and analyzing this process. I noticed that law enforcement never actually claimed that they had discovered drugs at the trailer. They simply stated that they had received reports of drug trafficking, that they were executing a warrant looking for said drugs, and that in the course of this raid they came under attack and four people were killed. So the incident was a "drug raid" gone bad, and that was that. I never did hear any one of them suggest that they owed any apology or sorrow for the people that they had killed.

I was a little surprised, trained as I was by old episodes of *The Night Stalker,* at the lack of inquisitiveness and simple initiative on the part of reporters. Over time, I realized that Miss Widdershins and Thomas simply had no constituency, no natural allies to plead their case. Their own people, the Dragons, were not going to raise questions; their chief concern, even now, was to avoid scrutiny, to keep what little they had, and to protect the King. There were no public interest groups that would take up their cause. They were not members of any publicly recognized marginalized community. They were not of any racial value. Quite the contrary, they were the universally despised 'trailer trash,' white supremacists, cop killers, and you'd be hard put to find anyone with a pole long enough to touch them.

Adrift in this sea of nonsense, I did note one thing that I thought might be of interest (and Dillon later confirmed this belief.) When they interviewed those chatty neighbors, one man conspicuously refused to talk. When the cameras came by, the man with the dead dog turned away and walked up into his house. There was a way he walked, with his face turned from the camera; he did not want to be seen, did not want to be thought of in connection with this event. It strengthened the suspicion I had, that here was the secret lying voice that had triggered this vile assassination. Indeed, we had all forgotten about him and his grievance too soon.

That was my time in the motel. It was only a few days, but by the time it was over I was sick of the room and the television, of hearing the same words and seeing the same pictures over and over. They had their story tied, wrapped and finished and they were content to let it lie.

4.

It was a few days before I thought to call my parents and tell them I was all right. I was reminded to do so by the sudden unexpected appearance of Easter. It was our first Easter apart, for I'd always come home from college for the holiday. Early Sunday morning I was surprised when the motel faction swept me out of bed and we drove off to Easter Mass together. Locked in the dreadful present moment, I'd forgotten all about the year's passage. It did me good to celebrate the Resurrection and death's final defeat. It did us all good, I think.

When I called my parents that evening, I was surprised to find that they needed no reassurance because they were completely unaware of the entire episode. My father and grandfather no longer watched the news every night, and even if they had done so there was no "hook" to this obscure Pennsylvania shootout that would penetrate the New York media cone of isolation.

Once I told them about it, of course, they became alarmed, and not just my mother. I could assure and reassure them that I was unharmed, but what had happened once could happen again and they knew it. They were enveloped in the same fear and uncertainty that had gripped us all, but I was very proud of them that they never asked me to come home, and did not ask if there was any truth in the accusations against my murdered friends.

Cornelia never did come to the motel to see me. It was considered imperative that she stay close to Arthur and that he be surrounded by the people he loved most and knew best. He'd decided to camp in the field where he could be with Fernando, his ailing pony, and Cornelia remained with him. Toward the end of the week, I started walking to the field each day to visit her and the others. She was very subdued. They had the place fairly well organized, a lot of tents laid out like an army camp, a lot of in and out traffic. They'd stayed there before and knew how to work the place. I'd never seen them in full gypsy mode, but I wasn't in any condition to make and record observations.

Cornelia spent most of her time with Arthur, an exhausting task even though there were plenty of others in attendance and he made no demands of any kind. Indeed, I never heard him utter a word.

I asked Cornelia, "How is he doing?"

"I don't know. I really don't know. Everything's changed for him. I can't tell how much he understands."

"He's so quiet."

"All the time. Not a word."

"How are you doing?"

"Sad. Just sad."

At last we got the "all clear" from Dillon to travel back to

Dragon Town. It had seemed a long time coming. First there were the autopsies, where the authorities had to document every wound, every entry and exit hole, to their satisfaction. Then Dillon had difficulties getting the bodies released for burial. There was no documentary evidence of kinship — there was no conventional documentary evidence of anything — and the authorities were in no mood to make things easy. Cassie had to drive to Pennsylvania first, and between her evidence — whatever pictures and letters Dillon deemed safe for public viewing — and Dillon's standing as a lawyer, they eventually broke the impasse.

We were all ready to leave by that time, even if it was only for a funeral.

5.

I sat at the back of the viewing room, one mourner of many, on one of a row of folding chairs set against the wall. The wake was held in a freestanding funeral home by the side of the main road, a little distance outside of town, with plenty of room for parking. Ours was the only wake being held, and it was a good thing, because the tribes came in their hundreds to pay respects. They had opened the wall between two adjacent viewing rooms, and I was actually at the back of the second room.

It was a departure from precedent, not holding the wake in Dragon Town. Dillon and Dinan waffled on the matter. They had to balance the current exposure of holding the wake in a public place against the long-term damage of attracting greater public interest in their permanent residence. They decided to brave public scrutiny now in the hopes of maintaining the town's obscurity, at that time and in the future. I think they were also influenced by the need to keep the poor battered bodies of the deceased in a place where they could be tended the last few days before going underground.

The tribes' old cars, trucks, vans and bikes were parked all over the lot, every which way, spilling on to neighboring grass, lining the side of the road. I knew there were scores of cars parked up at the field around the sun bower as well. Even though we tried to carpool over to the funeral home, so as to keep the traffic to a minimum, the place looked like some kind of civil defense crisis had hit town.

The size of the crowd had clearly alarmed law enforcement. The sinister separatist group of their self-justifying fantasies suddenly looked to be real. A local problem was no longer local. The white-trash, the expendables, the easily dismissed and forgotten cop killers were not so easily forgotten after all. Here were hundreds, thousands of people from all over the country coming to pay homage, here was a hitherto unsuspected, and therefore unregistered, uninvestigated, uncontrolled *movement* of some kind. Here was the unknown.

For us it was a disaster. There was a helicopter flying overhead, there were troopers walking the length and breadth of lot and roadside, taking pictures of license plates, taking pictures of people. Our motto had always been, "we see others and no one sees us," but now we were no longer invisible. When I walked into the funeral home in the late morning, in company with a full carload from Dragon Town, I had to pass a gauntlet of bald-headed steroid monkeys in flak jackets. We locked eyes, we glared, and I knew that here was another danger. The Dragons and the others were working themselves up to a furious pitch, I could feel it, and there were those among them no more likely to back down than Thomas himself. It wouldn't take much to set off an incident. The tribal leaders had actually detailed stewards, some of their older, more responsible members, to patrol the lower floor of the funeral home and the parking lot and streets, anywhere they saw men gathering to smoke and to talk, in order to calm the fiercer spirits and to smother sparks before they became fires.

About the only thing we had going for us was the lack of media presence. There were other stories breaking. A few days ago a royal wedding; and now, the first day of the wake itself, America's greatest enemy was reported killed, his body dropped in the ocean. There was little attention to spare for us.

So I sat sweating, shoulder to shoulder with my silent companions. I became aware of someone standing close to me, standing over me. I looked up and saw Cornelia, in a dark blue dress with a black armband.

"Come," she said. "I want you to sit next to me," and she took me by the hand and led me through the crowd.

She stopped to kneel at the coffin, and I knelt beside her, though I had already said my prayers. It was a double coffin and open, after a fashion. It was the usual half-door arrangement, but there was a kind of white gauzy veil across the open half, which partly obscured the two bodies beneath it. The overall effect was as if you were looking at two figures enchanted to sleep, who might sit up at any moment. The funeral home seemed to have done a remarkable job of piecing the two bullet riddled corpses back together, but I wondered if the filmy covering wasn't laid over them partly to conceal any inerasable effect of their violent deaths.

Cornelia and I rose, and turned; there were empty chairs up front waiting for us. Before we took our seats, Cornelia reached over the chairs to introduce me to a dark, middle-aged couple, Malcolm and Eileen Macpherson, whom she identified as the Chief of the Cats and his wife. It felt like a familiar wake scenario. They were like distant cousins whom you didn't know and couldn't quite place, but nevertheless liked very much; but even as you spoke with them you knew you wouldn't see them again until the next wake rolled around. Here there was even less inclination for small talk than at an ordinary wake, so in a few moments Cornelia and I took our seats with our backs to the rest of the room. Miss Widdershins' cousin Cassie was sitting on the far side of Cornelia. Mrs. Parsons was not there; I supposed she was with Arthur, while Cornelia took the opportunity to attend the wake.

Cornelia began to speak.

"Close in one grave, the two of them. Close as they lived. That is one mercy, the only mercy shown them. That one did not survive the other. A mercy to them, a misery to us. May they reach heaven together.

"Look at them, the two of them under a white sheet. Two sorrows I have had in my life. The loss of my father and the loss of my queen and my champion. Two sorrows. When my daddy died under wheels, it was then I went to Aunt Vivien. There could not have been a nobler lady or a sweeter companion. She helped heal my heart; who will heal me now?

"When the two of them lived, we had no fear of misfortune or malice. There were no terrors while Thomas lived. I have seen other men of weapons. There was none like him. When he struck once he did not strike again. Cut down naked by cowards in armor. Not one would have faced him in a lonely place."

"One is coming, two are coming," said Cassie. "He is not forgotten."

"Before he loved Aunt Vivien, he did not long for a feather bed. He preferred to lie on rushes by a running stream. He preferred a brisk fight under moonlight to a long soft lying in the late morning. Merry in court, a madness to our enemies. He was my fond uncle, a gentle patient soul. He was our prop, our strong wall. We had no fear while he lived. When they came, they came without honor. Unarmed he was taken by many. Another mercy: Though he was slain, he slew."

"One is coming, two are coming. He will not be forgotten."

"His love was given to Aunt Vivien. All our love went to Aunt Vivien. Our white flower, our lily, our font of joy. She gave with both hands, from her heart and from her treasure. Before you felt your need, Aunt Vivien would have given it to you. The house where Aunt Vivien lived was a house of peace, a house of mirth. I would rather drink cold water from a tin cup in her hall, than wine from cut crystal in any other. When men looked on Aunt

Vivien they lost speech. When she spoke, she banished confusion. Wisdom, beauty and kindness, was their ever such twining in one heart, in one body? She will be remembered forever. She will be remembered as long as Arthur."

Cornelia continued.

"God help their little son. We must all be fathers and mothers now. A hundred fathers, a hundred mothers, but none the proper one. A beautiful sapling, a perfect shoot, the last best son of the first best king. Who will protect him now? Who will protect him against the enemy that never sleeps?"

"One is coming, two are coming. There will be a reckoning."

I became aware that the other women were moaning in sympathy as Cornelia spoke.

"When last I saw Aunt Vivien she took me to her tent. There was wine for me if I wished it, there was cream and the sweet ripe berry. White in silver slippers, it was a wonder to see her, it was a joy to hear her. All the folk I loved best, under blue silk, under blue sky, for the last time together, although I did not know it."

The sighs of sympathy were almost like a song.

"One only was missing, Arthur the king, and that was a blessing, although I did not know it. The poor lame pony who kept him safe kept the line of the Dragons, although I did not know it. The pale cold hand, under white cloth, when I last saw it, was warm with giving. On each bestowing, in his degree, love's last gifts, although I did not know it..."

Cornelia kept speaking and the women kept up their sighing, but I cannot tell what she said, for she switched to their common

11. You Two

1.

For a week after the funeral, the mood at Dragon Town was one of stunned silence. It was the day after a hurricane, where we crawled out of the rubble and surveyed the damage under sunny scrubbed skies. Too early to act, too early to do anything but look. We were in limbo. We were on our own.

The funeral was held at the local church, the "vacation church" as I thought of it. It was small, so most of us had to stand outside. I sat inside with Cornelia, who sat beside Arthur. It was a difficult decision, whether or not to bring him to the funeral. There was great danger to his well-being; if the Bellymen recognized him as the orphaned child, it is likely they would have taken him and consigned him to child services. In the end we took the risk. We decided that it was important for him to participate in the ceremony. There was a sprinkling of other children in the congregation, enough that he would not be conspicuous. He sat and knelt in silence. He did not cry. He gave no clue what he was thinking, but he held close to Cornelia's arm the whole time.

The priest was not a local priest, but one of our own. He said the mass in Latin, old style. I doubt he had permission from the Bishop, since throughout most of the country using the Tridentine, the "Extraordinary," Rite was considered the equivalent of reciting *Mein Kampf* from the altar. Technically, he should not have needed special permission, given the lately issued *Summo-*

rum Pontificium, but that ruling was almost universally ignored. I'd heard a lot about that from my mother.

Before we left the church, Fr. Cleary sang to them, the deceased, two as one, the great song of the dead:

> *In paradisum deducant te Angeli;*
>
> *in tuo adventu suscipiant te martyres,*
>
> *et perducant te in civitatem sanctam Jerusalem.*
>
> *Chorus angelorum te suscipiat,*
>
> *et cum Lazaro quondam paupere*
>
> *æternam habeas requiem.*

We moved in a body to the burial ground. The hearse drove slowly and we walked, or rode, or drove alongside. There were more of us waiting at the cemetery. There were a large number of Geese in attendance, and I admired that, because I knew that many of them were in law enforcement or some sort of military service, and it might be a great black mark against them professionally to be seen at the rites of two such desperate cop killers. MacOwen himself was there, with his closest attendants. Throughout this whole ordeal and the hard work that followed, the Geese performed admirably. We have not forgotten.

It was a perfect day, the intimations of early summer; sunny, bright enough to make you squint, but the breeze blew long and soft and cool through the sibilant grasses. The burial took place at the Dragon's private ground, on the far side of their property, at the opposite end from the castle and a long distance away from the wells and the streams, as prescribed by law. The graveyard was bounded by an old black wrought iron fence, leaning in places as if tired from age. The grass grew long all around outside the fence, but it was soon trampled flat from the crowd. The coffin was brought to the hole. Fr. Cleary chanted, we prayed together, the Cat's piper played a long sweet air. But in the end, the coffin was lowered, and we all turned away, as we do at every funeral, bar the last.

2.

I spent some time with Fr. Cleary over the next few days. He was staying up at the Guard House with Mrs. Hughes and many others. He told me how the king, Miss Widdershins' father, had paid for his studies at the seminary. Looking at him, sitting at Mrs. Hughes' table, swallowing jars of coffee and burning through any number of cigarettes, comfortable among his own people, "in mufti," letting the shaving go for a few days, I thought how lonely he must be. It was hard enough to leave for those who were starting a family with a dedicated spouse, but what must it be to force oneself through seminary, struggling to absorb lessons on psychology and human sexuality, training for a life presiding over a "faith community" amid parish councils, liturgists, justice and peace committees, worship ministries, all the clamor and complaint of Bellymen? Suppose he had to deal with a school!

No one would understand him, not his flock, not his colleagues, not his confessor. He should have stayed with us. We could use a priest. But those days were over; the days when we had a stone chapel in the backyard. We were no longer a recognized community needing to be served. There was no trust and little love left. They were Bellymen first, churchmen second. I hope they found something for him, though, some life and some people he could connect to.

After a few days, Fr. Cleary left for home, one of many. One by one the far travelers, those who had come here to mourn, peeled away. About a week after the interment, it was noised abroad that there was to be held a council up at the castle. To my great surprise, Cornelia and I were both asked to be present.

When the day came and I walked alone through the center of town, I was stopped by Sarah, the little woman whom I had seen the day of the murder with her apron over her head, screaming. She had recovered from her extravagant grief to all outward appearance, and carried on her life and her duties, quietly, soberly, like the others, giving the impression of a windup automaton. The whole town went through the motions like figures on an old Swiss clock, wound and directed by Mrs. Hughes.

She stopped me and asked, "Are you going up to the castle?" for it was commonly known that there was to be a great council that day.

"Yes."

She looked towards the gate and the top of the keep where it could be seen over the wall, and said, "The hive without a queen."

"Yes."

"God support the young king, poor little boy."

I had learned a great deal about grief, about the varieties and gradations of grief, over the past few years. Every grief is different, its own unique emotion, grief for a child, grief for a friend and cousin, grief for a parent, grief for a sovereign and protector. I saw, what I could not have known, that grief for a king or queen, a true hereditary monarch, the bones and blood of the nation, was a very different thing from grief for the head of state in a democracy, where every elected leader is a despicable enemy to one faction and a disreputable ally-of-convenience to another. All the more so when the dead queen was known and loved personally by her subjects, a true mother. I saw too that there are as many individual griefs as there are individual people, each with his own particular love and loss. The world is a veritable tapestry of irreplaceable, irreducible griefs.

When I entered the courtyard above the town, I was surprised to see a familiar figure loitering about the gate with his back toward me. I had not seen Balin since he exited the car with Arthur and his retinue into the field at the gypsy camp. I hadn't seen him at the wake or the funeral, or in town afterward, and his absence had been unsettling to me, though I couldn't say why.

The figure turned toward me, and at first I was shocked how much he had changed in a few short weeks, though I would be hard put to say how. The coloring, the demeanor — he seemed sadder and older, redder and less physically challenging. Then I realized I was looking at Balan, his twin brother.

He shook my hand.

"I heard you were back," he said.

"Yes," I said. "I came back last year."

"I was up in Nova Scotia. I've been living with the Gaels up there for a while. I came back because of all this."

"Yes."

"Are you going to the council?"

"Yes."

"Don't let me keep you."

Neither he nor his brother attended the council. The part they would play had already been decided.

We trailed into the keep and up the winding stairs, we few. Everyone seemed reluctant. The council was to be held on the second floor. In addition to the seats at the round table, there were chairs set against the wall, for the overflow. I sat in one of these; it may have been the very chair upon which Arthur stood, less than a year ago, talking to the birds.

The two lawyers, Dillon and Dinan, sat together at what would have been the head of a rectangular table. They would be directing proceedings, now at the conference and for the foreseeable future. Cassie sat at the table as well, and her husband, Duncan. There was Mrs. Hughes and Garn, a number of people from out of state, unknown to me, and to my surprise, Dolores. Like me, Cornelia sat in a chair against the wall. Her mother was not there; I assumed she was with Arthur. Mattheus sat against the wall as well, and a couple of the artisans from town; the smith was there.

These were the people who would take care of the nation. The nation needed care; I understood that more after seeing the Dragons who came to the burial. She had been the judge, the benefactor, the protector, the hand that bestowed gifts and warded off misfortune. They were all worried about the future, for the first time facing it without the Pendragon. There were practical questions, where money would come from when they needed it, who would arrange a move and a new home when it was time to leave quickly, who would find a doctor, a lawyer, a soldier; who would deal with the other tribes on their behalf and keep them invisible to the Bellymen. There were other needs as well, more difficult to fill; who would keep their memory, who would renew their joy? Seated in this room were the people who would make these determinations, and I sat among them.

It was time to begin. Dillon rose from his chair. He rested his hand on a stack of papers. He and Dinan had several such stacks placed deliberately in front of them. We looked to him expectantly, but he faltered. I had never seen him lose command of himself before, and I doubt anyone else in the room had seen it either. I thought he was exhausted. Over the past few weeks, he had not only to take over the headship of the Dragons, both here in town and across the country, but also to deal with the civil and criminal demands of Bellyman Law. The Geese had lent him Stokowsi, the Haitian lawyer I knew from the old days, but although he pitched in with a will, he could not help with internal matters. They had even enlisted me to help with proofreading; years of reproducing Latin texts and double-checking notes and bibliographies for errors in form had given me a good eye. It was the closest I would ever come to taking over the tribe's legal work, but I didn't know that at the time.

So we sat and waited, Dinan with his head swiveled round, looking up at his colleague like a concerned bird, while Dillon said nothing, groping, it seemed to me, for words.

Then Dolores spoke, and she did not ask for permission.

"I see defeated eyes, I see long faces. Is it that we have forgotten? Is it that we have forgotten who we are and what is our road to tread? Have we lived so long in this fine, fat, generous country, in peace and in freedom, that we have come to believe in our place here, that it would go on forever, that we had nothing to do but whip cream for our coffee and drip honey in our tea. Have we forgotten that our place is the weedy lane, the highways and byways? That our kingdom is the in-between, hard won and hard kept, that our rest is the road. Or is it that we are afraid? Afraid of the new world, of the new man, the man without a soul, afraid to face the new world without our Queen, my poor lost poppet, and without our champion, the great warrior. Take heart. I mind the day when the kingdom was reduced to three, a man, a woman and a child, three in a cave with the sound of the sea in their ears, a man, a woman and a child, and the child was sick. And yet we prevailed. We still have what we had, the only possession we have ever had, our faith, our faith in the line, in the kingdom that never dies, our faith in each other, the faith that has never been broken. We still have our love, the love the knits us into a family, *Cenel Artuir* the everlasting, our love for one another, for the kingdom, our love for the king and the descendant of the Great King. We still have the heir, the successor, the king of the western isles, my little Arthur, my dear little boy, the hope of the nation to bring us back our joy and our glory. Take heart. We have what we always had, the only possessions we ever had. We are what we always were — what we have been, what we are now, and what we will forever be.

Quondam, nunc, futurus. Take heart. Remember and take heart."

She stopped talking.

The spell was broken.

We began.

3.

In the next few hours, I learned a great deal about the structure of the Dragon's kingdom. I hadn't known or imagined that there *was* any structure. I'd spent all my time at the Dragon's court, under the direct oversight of the monarchy, so I had no notion of how affairs were arranged across the larger tribe.

The kingdom was divided into districts, apparently, *provinciae* that were more or less geographically based. Most of the unfamiliar people seated round the table were district leaders, called *comites*, in what seemed a peculiar mixture of terms from different time periods. The *comites* received their authority entirely from the monarch, the Pendragon, and they could be appointed, removed and replaced entirely at the monarch's pleasure. Yet, from what I heard, many of these *comites* were the children and grandchildren of earlier office holders, so there seemed to be some sort of hereditary component to the office. Perhaps it was just natural for the Dragons to turn everything into a hereditary office, to keep everything within a family in absence of a compelling reason not to.

I wondered later how old the arrangement was, and concluded that, despite the Roman-sounding names, it must be fairly new. I couldn't see much reason for a provincial structure when they were gathered close together in the Isle of Man, or Argyll or Aileach or wherever else they had happened to settle in a body. It must have been when they went abroad to Europe and scattered over the European kingdoms and later over the Americas, it must have been then that they adopted this arrangement. I don't know why they settled on the archaic names; perhaps they were memories preserved from the old days in Britain, perhaps they got it all out of the Black Book.

The first part of the meeting was concerned with the lawyers giving new standing orders — the new military doctrine in effect — for managing the provinces and dealing with the Bellymen, the eternal and newly awakened enemy. I thought it was plain that there had been smaller meetings before this one, and that what was being publicly discussed now had already been privately debated and agreed upon. I heard a lot of particulars mentioned — particular people, particular places, particular laws — that meant nothing to me. What I got from it was that there was to be a general tightening of purse strings and a moratorium on alienating property. There were to be no more mid-month audiences either, such as I had first seen back in Queens, when Miss Widdershins would receive a stream of subjects suing for favors, most of which she was in the habit of granting.

Dillon stressed also the necessity of keeping meticulous track of anyone who fell afoul of the law.

"*Habeas corpus* is a dead letter," he said. "For the first time in a long time. We are facing a new legal landscape. It started with suspected terrorists and foreigners, and now the attitude has permeated the entire legal system. New violations are invented out of whole cloth and applied *ex post facto*. Anything might be a crime and anyone can be held indefinitely, on a new charge or on no charge, as long as the people can persuade themselves that public safety is threatened. Think of it as highly organized mob justice. It is imperative that we keep track of everyone, all our people, no matter what authority they fall under, no matter what iron hole they are put into. No one is forgotten, no one is abandoned, no one is lost. Everyone must feel confident of that."

The two worked the meeting as a tag team. Dinan took the lead. Everyone was to get ready to move at a moment's notice. Old routes and old refuges, some of which hadn't been used for decades, were to be opened up once again. Already the lawyers had begun the process of re-establishing contacts overseas.

"We must test the temper of our old friends in this new world. We must ascertain how much of the old loyalties hold true. I take nothing for granted. Duncan has kindly consented to go over to Europe for us. He knows the place best."

Dinan looked about the room and tapped his pen on the table.

"We must lose no time. Many, if not most of you, know that Balin is determined to exact vengeance when he can find the parties responsible for our Lord and Lady's murders. The Geese have promised help, but they can only walk a short distance down that road with us. Some of those who must pay will be federal or local law enforcement agents. There will therefore be a conflict of interest, perhaps even a conflict of sympathy among the Geese. And Balin is determined on vengeance in the old way. He will not be dissuaded."

I sensed not exactly a collective gasp but a definite reaction to this last bit of news. I was perplexed and looked over to Cornelia. She saw me, and I gestured with open palms as much as to say, "What is that, the old way?"

Cornelia spoke aloud.

"Heads on branches."

She must have seen skepticism or a reluctance to believe in my face, because she reiterated. "I mean it. Like Conall the Victorious after Cú Chulainn."

Dinan picked up from her interruption.

"When they start finding headless bodies, they will remember us, and all the people they photographed and filed and arranged at the funeral. They will come after us hard. But, as Dolores reminded us it will not be the first time. We have at least a year and a day grace period, probably longer than that, as it will take time for the Twins to find out what they need to know. But when the time comes our enemies will come after us hard and our arrangements must already have been made."

"But right now," he said, "our great task is the safeguarding and care of Arthur, our little king. This task must be approached with great delicacy of feeling. There are those here among us who spend the most time with him and who are closest to him, and the reports I have received indicate that they are without exception worried about him. For a child so young — for any child — losing both parents is a great sorrow, a lifelong sorrow, but the way Arthur lost his parents — they simply disappeared from his life

— is a particularly hard one. It is difficult to explain to him. We told him how they were taken, lest he spin fantasies in his mind, lest he think they had left him or that he had caused their deaths by not being with them. It is difficult to know what goes on in the mind of a child. Maybe he even blames us. Arthur was always close-mouthed, but now they tell me he has ceased speaking entirely. We must give him stability and trust. Stability is the great thing. We must surround him with the people whom he loves and who love him most. We must create again a loving family for him. Cornelia, we owe particular thanks to you and your mother in this regard, for the care you have taken of him."

"Oh … we help each other, my little Arthur and me."

I knew now why Cornelia was here, I thought. I assumed I must be here to gather background, to be "put in the picture" as they say; I would be helping the lawyers soon.

"We don't expect to bring Arthur back here to Dinas an Dragain. There are too many memories, he will be expecting to see his parents around every corner. Perhaps that is a wrong judgment, but it is one that must be made, one way or the other. In the short term we will take him on the road, which he has always enjoyed. In the long term, we have hopes of a solution, but we are not at liberty to discuss them yet. We will be moving our center of operation as well. I think we can assume that this place is under some level of surveillance. In a few weeks Dillon and I will be going to the southern hall in the hills. Communication will go through there. The townsfolk will remain here under the direction of Mrs. Hughes. That is all I can think of for now. The next years will be difficult. We must be patient, until Arthur is ready to take his rightful place. We must keep our faith, *fides gloria nostra.*"

"We will now address any questions," said Dillon.

I didn't pay much attention to the questions. I was thinking, if Arthur is going on the road then Cornelia will be going with him. But what about me? Was I to go south with the lawyers to the "hall in the hills," dotting i's and crossing t's? When would I see her again?

4.

The meeting was at an end. The councilors gathered at the head of the winding stairs, patiently waiting for their turn to descend. Cornelia and I stood together at the back of the pack.

I felt a tug at my sleeve. It was Dinan.

"I wonder if you two could wait behind with us for a few moments. We have a couple of questions to ask you."

I saw that Dillon was hanging back, and that Cassie was still at the table, and her husband Duncan, along with Dolores and Mrs. Hughes and a couple of the *comites.* Cornelia and I took our places. As we sat down, we shared one sideways glance, long enough for each to convey bafflement. Then we each sat in silence, looking straight ahead.

The last of the after-meeting conversations was over, the winding stairs were cleared, and Dillon and Dinan resumed their seats at the head of the table. They were looking at me and Cornelia now, and there was an uncharacteristic fondness, even an archness, in their gazes that I found disconcerting.

"Now," said Dillon. "You two. Cornelia, you have heard us talk about the good you have done for Arthur, and the attachment he has formed to you. We were hoping that you would take on the primary role in his care, that is to say, that you would be in effect a second mother to him."

"You would, of course, have the whole support of the kingdom," said Dinan. "Dolores would continue as his nurse, and your mother would, we hope, travel with you, and all of us would pledge life and liberty and love to the king and his caretakers."

I was beginning, at last, to see where all this was leading.

"You have heard us talk about the importance of stability for Arthur, and that means a stable family," said Dillon. "That prompts us to ask a question that we would not normally presume to ask. But the welfare of the king has been placed in our hands, the life of the whole dynasty has been reduced to a slender thread, and it has fallen to us here sitting at this table to see that it remains unbroken. So we must speak where we would ordinarily remain silent, where in ordinary times courtesy would demand silence. With that in mind, I presume to ask you two, what are your plans for the future? Do you have plans? I know you are young, but we have become so accustomed to seeing you together that I think we have all made assumptions, perhaps unwarranted..."

Neither Cornelia nor I spoke. I could feel myself growing red, with all eyes on us, and I was sure Cornelia was doing the same.

Dillon had another try.

"Again, I understand if you have not discussed such matters..."

"Oh, for goodness' sake," Dolores cut in. "Are you two going to get married?"

Dillon began to protest, but the question was posed, and alarmed though I was — my ears were singing and I knew my eyes must be bulging — I suddenly saw opportunity looming behind the confusion, an unexpected opportunity that must be grasped.

"We haven't discussed it," I said. "But yes I have hoped that Cornelia and I would get married one day."

I was afraid to look toward Cornelia, but this was not the time to give in to fears, so I forced myself to turn. And there Cornelia was beaming bright, and red, and moist, and she said,

"Yes, I hoped so too," and then she took my hand.

It was surely the strangest proposal in all the long history of the kingdom.

"Excellent," said Dillon, and the people cooed and came round us to congratulate us.

Dolores alone remained seated and declared to the empty table, "*I* knew they were going to get married eight years ago."

When they had all settled down, Dinan took up the reins of the meeting.

"We had hoped that you two would consent to serve as the guardians of young Arthur, as his adoptive mother and father. It is a solemn charge, as you know, and a great honor, the greatest honor there can be among us. As we have said, the whole energy, the heart and soul of the kingdom would be united with you..."

And he went on for a while. My head was spinning, I could have sworn the room was actually revolving, and I thought about the change that had come over my life in the span of an instant. I had gone from an aimless ex-college student to a married man with a ready-made family, and moreover to the bearer of a sacred charge, unique in all the world. I had my life laid out before me, I had my purpose, and I had my Cornelia, never to part.

Dinan came to a halt after not too long. After settling the great question, they did not pursue the details, the dates, times and places, leaving that for Cornelia and me to settle. As I sat watching them file out, and still holding on to Cornelia's hand, I quailed for a moment, thinking of the trust they were placing in me. I hoped it was not misplaced. I was a man of no accomplishments, I thought, save a little Latin and less Greek. Hardly the man to replace Thomas the Rhymer and guide the king. The one thing, the only thing I had to recommend me was that they knew I would keep faith with them, with Cornelia, with Arthur, with all of them, forever.

12. New Life

1.

A little more than a year later, I was back living in Queens. We moved into the Big House, the same place Cornelia and Miss Widdershins had been living when I first met them, only a few blocks away from my parents' house. It had been decided that it would be a good idea for Cornelia and me to be living close to my family, and I had no wish to argue. We brought the menagerie with us, Arthur, Dolores, Mrs. Parsons and a shifting assortment of officers and guards.

When we got to the front steps and prepared to enter the porch, Cornelia quailed. She took my arm and leaned against me. I hadn't considered that it might be difficult for her to move back to the place where she had lived with her beloved aunt. It hadn't occurred to her either, she later told me. But we pressed ahead and walked in, Arthur first, and the baggage brought in behind us. I remembered the smell of old wood, the characteristic smell. The house had been occupied during the interim by at least one family, and most of the old furniture was gone. There were childish paintings all over the walls in the basement, like brand new cave drawings, made just for us. Oddly enough, the bullet damaged brass lamp was still at the foot of the stairs, a memory of the day the Art Thief had tried to steal the Dragons' Vermeer, and it was sitting on the same side table.

After a very few days, Cornelia became reconciled to the

move. After a couple of weeks she told me, "I'm glad we're back."

Arthur had no associations with the house. He explored the cupboards in the kitchen, poked around in all the rooms upstairs. He selected his own room, the very room, it happened, where his mother had slept all those years ago. There was nothing of hers from the old days to draw him there, nothing that I could see. Perhaps it was some invisible essence left behind, some physical manifestation of memory that attracted him. Perhaps it was simply the nicest, brightest room in the house.

Cornelia and I took her old room, and we set to making the place a home again. It was very different from the places we'd lived in the past year, and I worried whether Arthur would take to a settled life in the city. There was no use asking him.

Only once he volunteered an opinion, a question really. It was night, and he wandered out the front door and off the porch and stood on the lawn looking up at the sky.

"Where are all the stars?" he asked.

I saw stars, the stars I was used to from childhood, whatever hardy points of light could penetrate the city glare. But for Arthur, who was used to the whole bright stretch of God's heavens, it was but a poor display.

We had been living under the sky for the better part of a year. Our wanderings, which might have looked aimless to an outsider, proceeded along a well-worn migration path, with safe harbors along the way where friends waited to receive us. The fields that we camped in, for the most part, were familiar to my companions, used for generations. I learned as I went. But things were changing, as more land was closed off and as the sleepless lidless electronic eyes watched more and more.

Mrs. Parsons instructed me.

"It's not how it was," she said. "It's artificial, to be honest, our going to and fro like this. You can't make a living on the road anymore. People don't want to hire us for transient labor. They'd rather hire aliens, now that there's a permanent population of aliens, all organized into permanent work crews. They don't trust us, when we show up at their door with our tools in a sack. They'd rather hire someone from the yellow pages. Thank God for real estate, for our old fixed property, or we'd be in a bad way."

We moved in fluid groups, with families joining up and branching off at will. Cornelia stayed with Arthur and I stayed close to Cornelia. Arthur lived with Cornelia and her mother in their big trailer and I latched on to any other groups with room in their cars, tents or campers. I finally learned to drive for real, though I still didn't have my license. It was a strange life for me, but I approached it without expectations. It was no stranger than college had been, really. When old Colin joined us again, I spent a lot of time with him, in his truck.

Cornelia and I finally got married by Fr. Cleary down in Florida. My immediate family was in attendance, my parents and my sister, but no one else from my side. It was a very small wedding party all around, very different from the great affairs that were *de rigueur* on Long Island. It had been difficult to arrange, between our travels, my parents' flight and lodging requirements, and Fr. Cleary's availability. We skipped the whole business of the six month "pre-Cana," we just stood up in church, early in the morning when no outsiders were around, and made our vows. I don't know how many regulations Fr. Cleary was bending or breaking, I don't even know if we ever got a real valid civil marriage certificate, but I do know we were well and truly married, and that is what mattered to us. It was an event of no outward distinction, but it was the fulcrum around which my life turned and keeps turning.

My family was happy enough, I thought. At least they were reconciled to my change in life. At the wedding reception, looking at my mother chatting with her neighbors, I thought again what a pity it was that she never got to know Miss Widdershins. In my mind's eye I could see the two of them, heads together, talking over cake. They would have gotten along. I thought that my mother had brought herself to the point where she knew that there was no use fighting, what would happen would happen, and she was leaving it up to God. I'm sure it had taken her, and therefore my father, a lot of worry and suffering and anguish to get there. In the end, the sight of Cornelia, my bride in a white dress, sailing serenely over, through and around the proceedings, should have been enough to calm and charm any new mother-in-law.

Our honeymoon was short and sweet. They drove us to a cottage by a lake and left us there for a few days. Before our wedding, Cornelia had to spend some time assuring Arthur that she was not disappearing, that she would be back very soon. He was very clingy with her and was often seen walking with one hand holding on to Cornelia's and the other carrying his crazy little

Madeleine Trotter puppet.

We only had a few days in our pine-shrouded cabin before we rejoined the others. I moved into the big trailer with Cornelia, her mother and Arthur. It was hardly an ideal lodging for a newly married couple, but not so different, and certainly not worse, than when couples married during an Atlantic crossing in the old days, or under conditions of siege. I was determined to be grateful for what I had, but still I was happy when after a few months the suggestion was made that we move back to the Big House.

Looking back on the life now, I remember most vividly the late late evenings before we all turned in for bed, the smell of the dying fire, the single pure line of the last slow tune of the night, the low contented murmur of voices, and silent above us the great eternal wheel of the sky. So we understood what Arthur was missing, Cornelia and I, and a few nights after he named the lack of stars we took him out to the park, in the hopes that we could show him a better panorama. We stood in the best clearing we could find, shielded by trees from the standing lamps, across which we had once run, pursued by police cars, now nine years ago. Arthur dutifully looked up at our prompting, but even here the dominant glow of the city shoved aside nature's glory. When I was Arthur's age I would have thought it a brave show indeed, but he knew better.

I stood and watched them for a while as Cornelia waddled him back homeward, Arthur silent as always. The stars were one more loss in his life, like his parents, like his poor little pony who finally succumbed to age, like the castle, like the road. An owl called, and I thought of one of the poems I'd heard the Dragons recite around the fire, "what is the bird's song but a reminder of what is gone?" That was how it seemed with Arthur, and I didn't know what I could do about it.

2.

We worked with him over the following months. We took him to watch sailing ships, the little white ships in the bay and the tall ships coming in from the Sound. We took him to parades. We took him to the beach, to play in the waves. I wanted him to feel that his new home had promise. Everywhere we went he followed along obediently. You never had to tell him anything twice. He never complained. He never said anything. It was impossible to tell what he was thinking. Perhaps he had learned that whenever he showed love for something it would be taken away from him. If we were the type of people to have dealings with psychiatrists, we might have taken Arthur to see one, in the hopes that he might have seen such things before.

We took him to story time at the local library. He sat on the floor with the other children. He looked like a bear cub set amongst puppies. I don't think anyone believed he was six years old. Cornelia and I watched from the margins hoping he would connect with one of the others. It seemed hopeful at first; he seemed to be striking up some sort of wordless comradeship with a little black boy seated next to him on the mat. But after the session was over, the energetic story-teller passed around activities booklets to the children so they could continue the fun at home. Arthur took his as he would a napkin, with no interest in the markings on it, and when the story-teller tried to show him how to use it, he simply sat and looked at her.

"He doesn't read yet," Cornelia explained and was rewarded by a spontaneous movement, a little backwash as the other parents and even the children drew away from us. Most of these kids, I suppose, had been in school for three years already.

A mother, and then another, began to — I might almost use the word — *remonstrate* with Cornelia urging the vital necessity of teaching her young child to read ASAP. Cornelia, irritated, snapped, "What makes you think *I* can read?" and that was the end of it. She was decked out in full gypsy mode, the silver and the earrings, in heels that put her well above six feet, and no one wanted to risk a confrontation.

I was proud of her for that and proud of her later when a librarian drew us aside to a secluded nook and shyly began telling her about adult literacy programs. She took no umbrage, but recognized that the librarian was trying to be helpful, and responded, "Oh, isn't that kind of you."

Afterwards she had some trouble putting the librarian off. We didn't want to leave any contact information, of course, but Cornelia was reluctant to admit that she was already literate lest the librarian think we were making game of her. In the end, Arthur provided her escape. He'd had enough and he simply walked out the double front doors to the busy sidewalk and we had to hurry after him. He never did make friends with that little black boy.

I related the anecdote to my father the next day, with my

grandfather listening.

"What's the hurry?" asked my grandfather.

"Let him live as a child as long as he can," said my father. "Flann O'Brien said that the illiterate man experiences the world directly, without mediation. When we meet such a person we should let him go his own way instead of trying to reform him."

My grandfather spent a lot of time with Arthur. He was oblivious to any problem, only remarked on what a good-natured, tractable child he was. The two of them made a good pair. They spent many hours together over at my parents' house, my grandfather seated on the couch staring away into space or into the past or wherever. As his mind retreated into itself, his eyes became little black buttons, like a doll's sewed-on eyes. Wherever my grandfather went in his long periods of silence, it must have been somewhere pleasant. He always seemed serene, and Arthur was serene while my grandfather was with him. Arthur sat on the floor and played with a set of wooden blocks that had belonged to my father, and each took great comfort in the other's presence, although neither spoke. It was a dynamic more common with two-year-olds than with children of Arthur's age, or so said my parents.

Sometimes my sister would add herself to the mix and play on the piano the old favorites that my grandfather loved:

Tell me the tales that to me were so dear,

Long, long ago, long, long ago,

Sing me the songs I delighted to hear,

Long, long ago, long ago

The music brought him back from his interior wanderings and he would smile and sing along.

Whatever explanations my parents had made to our extended family about my sudden marriage and the lack of a full normal wedding with a reception, I was mercifully far away when they were making them. Probably they played up the gypsy angle. Probably, my extended family were not entirely displeased that they would not have to travel God knows where to meet God knows who and sit for hours being entertained by God knows what. When I came back to Queens and started circulating amongst them again, they were duly impressed by Cornelia — and many remembered her from the cookout in the old days — but Arthur took some getting used to.

We told people he was Cornelia's nephew, whose own parents had been killed in an accident, which was true enough, up until the "accident" anyway. I had worried about fielding questions about the nature of his parents' death — should we tell people they were shot by law enforcement officers and open up that whole chapter to inquiry? — but as it turns out people did not press the question. At first I thought that, as usual, they simply weren't interested in what I had to say, but my sister suggested another explanation.

"You know they think Arthur is Cornelia's?"

"What?"

"They think Arthur is Cornelia's son. By a teenage indiscretion."

"Did they tell you that?"

"They asked me."

"What did you tell them?"

"I told them the truth. But they didn't believe me."

"Well, people can be stupid."

"They can indeed... But at least they can read."

"Yes, at least there's that," and we both laughed.

3.

It was the birth of our daughter that finally brought Arthur back. When Cornelia had recovered from her labor, they brought Arthur to her bedside. She was propped up on pillows. Arthur looked down with great interest at the tiny creature in Cornelia's arms, with her eyes scrunched shut and her mouth opening now and again in a feeble bleat of protest against this new unasked-for world. He had been prepared for the birth, of course, but even so, this new arrival was an amazing thing.

"That's your cousin," we told him.

"My cousin?" He considered. "What is her name?"

"We are going to call her Anne."

He nodded. An important moment. The world was finally giving where it had for so long only been taking.

"Anne," he said, and smiled.

The lead-up to Anne's birth had been nerve racking, but not for anything Cornelia did or said. She was probably the most placid among us, but even she began to show nerves as the day drew near.

"Man, I'll be glad when this is over with," she said. "Things can return to normal."

"Not really. They can argue about how to take care of her."

There were many women about, too many women about, although they were all very helpful and all very good and kind to Cornelia and all wanted only the best for her. Mrs. Parsons and Cornelia and Dolores too were settled on a home birth. That was the way they always did it in their set, and I doubt they thought much about it until my mother raised her objections. She thought the whole thing was ridiculous and dangerous.

"What if something goes wrong? What if she needs blood? They can take care of you in the hospital."

This made sense to me. When I thought of home births, I envisioned countless birthing scenes in movies and Western TV shows, with the father waiting outside, sweating and revolving his hat in his hands, and as often as not getting bad news.

Cornelia, I think, being new to this kind of thing, would have gone along with her elders whatever they advised, but her mother was determined. Mrs. Parsons and my mother conducted their dispute with icy politeness, but when my mother would get home after a session, she let would let loose freely, so my sister told me, while my father tried to calm her.

There were a few things that kept the argument from getting out of hand. For one thing, neither the Dragons nor the Cats had anything against medicine, and they were willing enough to bring Cornelia along in her pregnancy under a regular doctor's care. For another, when my mother contacted Aunt Denise, who was a nurse, she learned that home births were becoming "a thing," even fashionable again, and that there were procedures that had been developed to make the whole thing quite safe. Relatively.

My mother explained it at length to me and my father over at our house, ostensibly reassuring me, clearly trying to talk herself into a more equable state of mind.

She discussed the various options from obstetricians to midwives.

"They have something called a 'doula' who's not a doctor, but a sort of midwife..."

My grandfather looked up from the couch on which he'd apparently been dozing and made his one and only contribution to the question.

"Did you say 'doulā'? That means 'female slave' in Homer."

We let that pass and he returned to his twilight slumber.

My mother did achieve one compromise; she negotiated the presence of a professionally trained nurse, a family friend, as a midwife. There was quite a gaggle of women around Cornelia when she gave birth. I waited downstairs, and outside, and downstairs again, in a high state of agitation. Arthur came and sat with me, I remember, and looked up at me with concern, and even handed me Madeleine Trotter to calm me. So I suppose little Anne was calling him back to the world even before she was born into it.

In the end, it was a very easy labor, they said. Cornelia was as strong and as sound as a horse. That had always been our hidden ace, our secret weapon, no matter where the birth took place. I really don't know why they had been so dead set against a hospital birth. It might have been as simple as tradition, they wanted Anne born the way they had all been born. It might have been memories of Miss Widdershins' brother, the boy who should have been king but had died in a hospital misadventure. It might have been atavistic fear of the added layers of bureaucracy and security in hospitals, fear of bringing our sacred family into a veritable stronghold of Bellymen and trusting entirely to their mercy. For they do steal our children when they get the chance.

From the first moment he met her, Arthur appointed himself Anne's guardian. When I saw him standing by her crib, I was reminded of those old black-and-white pictures of bull terriers supposedly serving as "nanny dogs" for the family. We were on much safer ground with Arthur on the watch. Indeed, I'm not sure how much he trusted *us* to handle things without him. He was determined to see to it that we did right by Annie, and was always ready to call us to account when we seemed to be failing her.

I remember one typical occasion, when Cornelia was trying to put into effect a recommendation she'd seen in a baby book. She had picked the book out of a used book store, the only one left in walking distance, a tiny place, just about the width of a doorway on the main boulevard. I don't know how they stayed in business, but I was glad that they did. This book was probably decades out of date when Cornelia bought it, but I suspected she wanted something as a counterweight to all the advice she'd been receiving from her nearest and dearest. She wanted to find things out on her own and to do things her way, the way she had figured out and decided on herself.

Now Anne was a colicky baby who kept very irregular hours. We had enough people on hand that we could accommodate Anne's eccentric sleeping patterns without any one of us losing too much of our own sleep, but Cornelia wanted to try to put Anne on a regular schedule, as they recommended in the book. This involved sometimes at night *letting her cry herself to sleep,* and that is what we were attempting to do. Cornelia had told her mother and Dolores about her plan. They exchanged glances, but let her carry on. But no one had told Arthur.

So that night we lay in the dark listening to the piteous cries of our only child. With a great thud, our bedroom door was thrust open, and a sturdy figure stood in the doorway, a black silhouette against the hall light.

"It's Arthur!" said Cornelia. "Let's hide!" and she buried herself under the covers with a great rustling of linens and hair.

Arthur came over and stood by the bed.

"Baby's crying," he announced grimly.

I feigned sleep. I could hear Cornelia giggling under the quilt.

Arthur seized the bed and began shaking it roughly.

"Baby's crying," he repeated.

It was hopeless. He would not take no for an answer. I rose to attend to Annie, but it turned out she was hungry, and it was Cornelia she needed.

As Cornelia sat in the cozy chair nursing Anne, she said to me. "Och, who am I kidding? I couldn't have held out much longer anyway."

4.

In time, and not so very much time, Anne got over her colic. Cornelia and I derived a great deal of enjoyment from watching Arthur fuss over our daughter. We were two of a kind, I thought, Arthur and I. Just as he took care of Anne, it was my task to take care of him. I puzzled over our common consuming drive. People, not just the Brights but even ordinary people, talk a lot now about how parents produce and nurture children because they are programmed to pass on their genetic code. I never attached much credence to that. It's true that Anne was Arthur's cousin so I suppose it's possible that his DNA somehow magically recognized a connection to Anne's own, deep calling to deep so to speak. But I didn't have a drop of blood or a speck of code in common with Arthur, yet here I was caring for him not from duty alone, but just as much from love. I thought that it must be natural for human beings to care for the helpless children who were entrusted to them, something to do with us being the image and likeness of our creator. In Arthur, perhaps, the pattern was burned yet deeper, for he was a king back through fifty generations, and he was a guardian and protector to the bone.

So what was I to do with this king, this heir to the ages, this little boy running through my house holding a pink pig puppet by one hand? Who would teach him the things his father would have taught him? Who was there left to teach him the old swordsmanship? Balin might have done it, but he was away on business. Arthur and I hit each other with sticks, of course, but I didn't have the proper skill or knowledge to pass on. It's so easy for traditional skills to die out when a tribe gets small enough. One untimely death and an art centuries old is lost forever. It was the same with Dinan's lectures and poetry. Such things — for he composed poetry in the old style — require an art in the hearing as well as in the composing, and with Miss Widdershins gone there was no one left to pay the proper attention.

Most of all, I wondered who would teach Arthur how to be a king, now that Miss Widdershins was gone. I tried to find him stories, folktales, examples from history, that would, as they say, "model" kingship. I had trouble finding good movies and television programs to show him. Almost everything produced in the last thirty or forty or even fifty years that dealt with the topic — whether in print or on screen — portrayed the royalty and the known heroes of European history as fops, perverts, cowards and fools. I had my best luck with Korean TV series and Indian movies which I checked out from the library, though most of them weren't for children. They depicted the noblemen and gods of the old world with dignity and *gravitas*, even the villains, and they usually came with subtitles which I could read to Arthur. Incidentally, between the subtitles and Cornelia reading "Goodnight Moon" and the like to a growing Anne, Arthur at last took the notion that it might be fun to learn to read. He picked it up, it seemed to me, in a matter of weeks. And he didn't need to go to school eight hours a day to do it.

At last it came to me that it was his *people* who must teach Arthur to be king, just as it is our children who teach us to be parents. The way they acted toward him would teach him how to act toward them. It was one more reason to keep the visitors coming through, all kinds of visitors, some on business, some just to look in on their king. I encouraged them all, until eventually even Cornelia had enough: "Do we have to have all these *people* around all the time?"

It was good for Arthur, I thought, particularly when he saw familiar faces, people he knew from the old days. His people. Left to our own devices, we had too many women about the place. We needed to bring more of the tribe's men into the house. Such a pity Troll wasn't alive; he could have played with Arthur the right way. I did my best, but I was only one man. I was happy when our new bodyguard was assigned, and he was Dónall Óg, whom I'd spoken with in the gypsy camp before the funeral and whom I knew from the old days, a young fellow and friendly. He was occupied with his duties, and serious about them, but he often made time for play with Arthur. Siobhán spent a couple of months with us, another woman, but she brought her new son with her. He was very young and it was easy for Arthur to coopt him into his projects. Siobhán's husband was off travelling in the west and that disappointed me. I would like to have met him and to have seen what manner of man he was. I imagine Siobhán would pose a challenge to anyone.

The lawyers came through Queens on a few occasions — sometimes together, sometimes separately — and I learned more about the business of the kingdom, by degrees. We were in an ambiguous situation, Cornelia and I; we were not really officers of the kingdom with clearly delineated powers of decision, but we were the people closest to the king and therefore everything that touched him touched us. These were uncharted waters for everyone and we navigated the long *interregnum* together.

As for Anne, our comical beloved Anne, she was ours, all ours. I used to say, as the Romans used to say about satire, *Anna tota nostra est.* She was developing into a plump little chatterbox, with definite and unexpected ideas about the right way and the wrong way of everything, and she reminded both of us more than a little of her grandmother, the terrifying Mrs. Parsons. She grew and she toddled and her parents grew and toddled along with her.

So it went on for months stretching into years, until the word came through that Balin was ready to strike, and it looked like we would have to move again.

Epilogue

I am writing this sitting on a slow boat to Europe. We embarked a few days ago on a cargo ship that rents berths to passengers. I'm sitting on a deck chair, out on the little expanse of free deck set aside for passenger recreation. The others, Cornelia and the kids, Dolores and Dónall Óg, are somewhere below, taking a break from the sun.

I don't know what we're carrying. It's a container ship, and I don't understand the markings on the containers. I don't know where we're going. I know we get out at a French port, and I know someone will be waiting for us, but after that...? They will bring us somewhere out in the country, to a friendly house where we can stay in quiet for a while without anyone the wiser.

It was decided that we should take Arthur out of the USA, until Balin's vendetta had run its course. I am still not convinced by the reasoning behind it. The others, the council and the lawyers, thought it would be safer if Arthur was somewhere he couldn't be snatched suddenly. They hadn't been able to penetrate the cloud of secrecy surrounding law enforcement's investigation into the Dragons. They were laboring in the dark and they were worried. The Geese hadn't been able to help us at all with the Feds, and even with local police and sheriff's offices their sources weren't much good. Crux of the matter, we didn't know if they'd connected Thomas killed in Pennsylvania to Con Gone-Away killed in a Queens park eight years before. We didn't know if the New York police or the *federales* were keyed into us. The council decided they didn't want to take the chance, they wanted Arthur somewhere he couldn't be touched, physically. So we sailed.

We left like spies, smuggled into cars, dressed to hide our identities, some leaving from the house in the middle of the night, some picked up in broad daylight from the park, with their baggage packed and transported the day before. I thought it was fun, frankly, though I knew I would miss the house and the city.

To my surprise, Arthur, when he learned we were moving again, became quite anxious. He asked a lot of untypical questions, "Who is coming with us? Will people know where we are?" I tried to reassure him over time that we were travelling with our usual retinue, that others would join us, that we were going to live with friends. I showed him pictures of where we would settle, a very pretty place with lots of trees and horses. He became reconciled to the move, ostensibly, but I did feel that my words were somehow missing the point, missing what was really bothering him.

Cornelia, just before we left, came to me with a theory.

"I think he thinks they're coming back."

"Who?"

"Aunt Vivien and Uncle Tom. I swear. He wants to make sure they can find him."

"No. Really?" No one had made any secret of the fact that his parents were dead and gone. "Are you sure?"

"No. I'm not sure. But I get the impression. I've heard him speaking to Madeleine Trotter, and some of the things I've heard him say..."

"Maybe it's just make believe."

"Maybe."

"What should we do?"

"What can we do?"

I couldn't imagine taking the child aside and browbeating him with the death of his parents and insisting that he acknowledge it as final. That would be inhuman. We would have to let things run their own course.

It struck me that this was a new version of the old belief, in the once and future king, in the return of the golden age. Nothing so good and so noble and so loved could be gone forever. I saw hints of the feeling even in the others, a sort of golden dust sprinkled over the world, casting the glamor of the past over the bereaved present. I began to understand how the memory of a good king, a truly noble court, could knit a people together forever. Perhaps it was happening again, another legend growing to keep us strong for a thousand years.

My father was dubious about the plan to go to Europe. I had been most forthcoming with him, out of all our family, about our coming troubles, though I did not, could not tell him about the death of Con Gone-Away ten years ago, nor about Balin's planned vengeance for the murders of the Queen and her Consort. He did know that we were concerned about Arthur's safety and that we wanted to keep him with us and away from Child Services. He knew that we wanted to disappear.

"Why to Europe? If anything they're worse than us, when it

comes to bureaucracy. You'll need all kinds of papers. Why not just disappear somewhere in the United States, somewhere out West? They must have places."

"I don't know. They're not sure about the old places anymore. They don't want to test it with Arthur."

"You'll need passports."

"Mine is still good. They're getting Cornelia and Arthur passports from one of those second passport countries, down in the islands."

"That sounds expensive."

"Tell me about it."

"If you run into trouble in Europe, with your visa or whatever, don't forget the American Consulate. You're still a US citizen."

"I won't. They're just gonna stash us at an estate for a little while. It might be fun. Maybe they make wine."

My mother took the news surprisingly well. Of course, she dreaded the day her sunny little granddaughter would be taken out of her life, but after our return to the Big House and the birth of Anne there, she is now confident that we will always come home again. (She knows nothing about Balin.) Maybe she is coming to be like the others, believing in the Return, that lost happiness will one day be restored. My grandfather used to have a tag, *multa renascentur quae iam cecidere.* Many things will be reborn that now have fallen. Horace, I think. I can't ask him now. He passed away after a sharp gruesome illness following a fall. It was hard time and a great loss for all our family.

My sister wants to visit us when we get settled. I think she probably will. The boyfriend is long gone. He'd found a fellow musician with a better job than hers and with better credentials, to my sister's quite evident relief. She's still bored teaching school.

Balin came to visit us before he set off on his quest. He wanted to see Arthur again, and Cornelia as well. We were happy to welcome him, and after he and Arthur had finished roughhousing, and he had met Anne, and Arthur had shown him around the house — not realizing that Balin already knew it well — we all sat together for a while in the backyard.

Balin was glad to hear that we were going to Europe.

"Good idea," he said. "Get away from this country a while. This place … these rivers and valleys, these trees … There's nothing for us here, nothing that means anything. There's no spirit here. It's just matter. Sticks and rocks. Nothing alive. Even the towns, there's no history, no memory. Maybe there's something here for the Indians, but not for us. You should move back to the old country and see what you find. See if there are any of the old spirits left."

"It's changed, I think," said Cornelia.

"There must be something left. Go to the old places. See if you can raise the fairies." Balin laughed.

He watched Arthur playing in the backyard. He'd built a fort out of pinecones and pebbles and populated it with plastic toy soldiers.

"I don't suppose I'll see any of you again," Balin said.

I hadn't asked him any particulars about his plans or his targets, and he hadn't volunteered. I sensed strongly that he had a great reluctance to embark on his vendetta, that it was not so much grand passion that drove him, but rather duty. It was his responsibility, it was a task that needed to be performed and that would be performed properly, but I thought he would find little joy in the performance of it. Yet he would readily spend his life, and maybe his brother's too, in the execution of justice.

After he left I thought, there goes another friend that Arthur has lost.

Despite my misgivings about the reasons for the trip, I am happy to be going to Europe. In a strange sort of reversal, I imagine that my emotions are similar to those once felt by emigrants from Europe heading for the New World. Here is a chance to escape from the hatreds and madness of the old life and to go to a place where things are cleaner, more beautiful, more authentic. I don't know if it is my life with the Dragons that has darkened my perspective on the society outside our walls, but it seems to me that the country at large has changed for the worse over the past few years, and has become nothing but a mob in session every day all day. There is no reason, and no reasoning with anyone, only a slow-burning hysteria. It will be a relief to escape from that and to live for a while in a place where one's interactions with the Bellymen are strictly limited by language difficulties — I would like a croissant, where is the *Hotel de Ville*? *Un verre du vin rouge s'il vous plait.* Where any misunderstandings are genuine, not feigned for advantage. Simple, direct, real.

They're coming up on deck now, I'll have to stop writing soon. It's a beautiful sunny day with a nice breeze against the bow, called up by the forward motion of the ship. We're making good time. The sea is calm as a lake. Cornelia put Anne down on the white painted deck. We were worried at first about her toddling around the unfamiliar ship, since there are fairly minimal safety features for passengers, but Cornelia set Arthur to guarding her, and he's as good as a border collie hemming her in and keeping her safe. She's walking across the deck toward me, making the crazy sounds she likes, "brrumm, brrumm." She'll be in my lap soon. She likes to sit and draw on whatever I happen to be holding.

I'm down in our cabin, writing under the lamp. Cornelia is asleep; wherever she lies she still sleeps sound. The sleep of the innocent. Annie conked out too; she's breathing easy in the little crib we brought on board. It's a tiny cabin, very cozy for the three of us, but tiny. For a freighter, it's not a big ship. I can feel the engine throbbing; soon I'll be asleep myself. I keep thinking, and it's almost a mystery to consider, how this work-a-day ship that is not so very big, holds my family in its lap and the future of a kingdom. A few fragile lives trusted to the mercy of the sea and the strength of this not very big freighter. The heritage of centuries, the thousand-year legend, wrapped up in one little eight-year-old boy and cast onto the waves. Well, it's not for the first time.

I have learned that there is some good in being a generalist. There are things I can teach Arthur that perhaps no one else could. It will be interesting to see in what direction his mind develops. He has shown great interest in the engineering features of the ship. If he becomes a mathematician he will be on his own in short order as far as I am concerned. He has gone from an illiterate to a voracious reader in little more than a year. His favorite book is the old Golden Iliad and Odyssey, illustrated by the Provensons, Alice and Martin. He reads it to Madeleine Trotter. He has shown no signs of growing away from her.

I'll start him on Latin soon, great fun if you do it right and the door to an almost limitless world to wander. Give the oldest things to the youngest people, as my grandfather used to say. (G.K. Chesterton, I think.) I've also come to see the importance of songs in his upbringing, the old songs of his people. There's a whole emotional, aesthetic, moral, supernatural world in those songs. Sometimes I think if everything else was lost, even the Black Book, you could build up the kingdom again just from the old songs. I hope Mrs. Parsons comes over to join us before not so very long and sings for us again.

There's nothing more now to write. Nothing but for me to lie down and wait for sleep, and to wonder, as I have so often in the past, over how I came to be here and how I came to be tutor and guardian to the last lost king of the western isles.

Terence Gallagher lives in Queens, New York, where he grew up and to which he keeps returning. He studied classics, with a side of bagpiping, in Massachusetts, and medieval history in Toronto, and spent a dozen years or so as an academic librarian, mostly in southwest Florida. He has published short stories and poetry in small journals in the US and UK. This is a second novel, a sequel to *Lowlands*.